OPERATION RIMBAUD

JACQUES GODBOUT
OPERATION RIMBAUD

TRANSLATED BY PATRICIA CLAXTON

Cormorant Books

**Canada Council
for the Arts** **Conseil des Arts
du Canada**

The publisher gratefully acknowledges the support of the Canada Council for the Arts
and the Ontario Arts Council for its publishing program. We acknowledge the
financial support of the Government of Canada through the Book Publishing
Industry Development Program (BPIDP) for our publishing activities.

Printed and bound in Canada

Library and Archives Canada Cataloguing in Publication

Godbout, Jacques, 1933–
[Opération Rimbaud. English]
Operation Rimbaud/Jacques Godbout; translated by Patricia Claxton.

Translation of: Opération Rimbaud.
ISBN 978-1-897151-22-8

1. Claxton, Patricia, 1929–. II. Title.
III. Title: Opération Rimbaud. English.

PS8513.02606313 2008   C843'.54   C2008-903726-X

Cover design: Angel Guerra/Archetype
Author photo: © All rights reserved
Translator photo: Larry Assam
Inerior text design: Tannice Goddard/Soul Oasis Networking
Printer: Marquis

CORMORANT BOOKS INC.
215 SPADINA AVENUE, STUDIO 230, TORONTO, ON CANADA M5T 2C7
www.cormorantbooks.com

OPERATION RIMBAUD

Biarritz, May 1967

1

BEFORE WE BEGIN, LET'S SAY this is a sulphurous story, it
smells of the devil, stale volcanoes, wooden matches, those
lemon yellow pyramids beside factories, sulphuric acid baths.
You say most people can't tell the difference between the
smell of sulphur and the smell of rotten eggs? All right, so
this story smells of rotten eggs. You'll have to hold your nose
if you want to hear it. Anyway, here I am this morning,
writing something sacrilegious, satanic, scandalous. I've put
away my incense burner, I've had it with ceremonials.

Through the window of my room overlooking the ocean,
all the way to the far side of the bay, there are valiant souls
pushing their surfboards out to sea. The picture comforts
me, tells me I'm not the only token Sisyphus on earth. If it
takes my last breath, I'm going to tell all with what I'm
writing. Adieu, do-gooders!

I had to withdraw from the world in order to write and protect my backside. Having no particular liking for mountain retreats, miraculous grottoes, or Dominican monasteries, I chose this hotel, where I'm as anonymous as I choose and don't risk running into stooges. It's a luxury I can treat myself to before perhaps ending up in the morgue.

I arrived here with my backpack, a long beard, and a credit card. From the minute you enter, the Hôtel du Palais in Biarritz offers you an atmosphere of calm in a spacious lobby that's scented with jasmine and softly hued. The tiny receptionist behind her walnut counter is particularly comely, her face magnificently made up. The porter, to the left near the elevators and grand staircase, is reliably as deferent as a Swiss banker. Modern comfort in a nineteenth-century setting is found here. Indeed, this once was the palace of Napoléon III and the Empress Eugénie. It was turned into a casino, then into a luxury hotel for crowned heads, was burned down, rebuilt, then occupied during the war by the Germans, who assuredly had less fun than the movie stars after the Führer's defeat. This is a huge building of painted brick in the purest "English castle" style. They say that the Duke of Windsor and his duchess felt at home in this hotel. As for me, I feel at home anywhere. Content in some tiny cell, comfortable in high society. I'm a barely domesticated animal, an alley cat that knows how to behave.

The idea of taking up quarters in Biarritz came to me when I learned from *Paris Match* that the Emperor Hailé

Selassie, the Lion of Juda, had spent several weeks here after I had met him in Montreal in March. We have since become bosom buddies, if I may say so. His Majesty had left Canada for Europe, and I thought he was back in the capital of Ethiopia as agreed, whereas he was really bathing with his court and drowning his fleas in the hotel's huge open-air pool. You can't trust anyone anymore.

Officially, I work for the Company of Jesus, which is why at times some people call me "Father Larochelle," despite my mere thirty-five years and my professional celibacy. But I have a feeling this is not going to last. I've pushed the door of the fourth dimension rather hard. The Company is a convenient cover for a certain number of clandestine activities, the most important of which is, and has long been, exchange-rate speculation: the network is flawless. Also in our ranks we have conscientious missionaries preoccupied with heaven and hell. These have heard the call of the true vocation and do not sleep curled up, ears cocked, in big soft beds that once belonged to the Empress Eugénie, whose initials adorn the garden and the salmon pink wallpaper.

Papa would have loved this place. He had only one big regret when he died — not to have joined a religious order in time to take off to Mexico with the coffers. "Just think, Michel," he often said, tossing back a swig of beer, "of all the land the Sulpicians own, plumb in the middle of Montreal!" He had observed that these Gentlemen of Saint Sulpice were fewer and fewer in number, and more and more senile. Child's play, a few accounting entries and light would have shone upon our lives. My father was not a loser, but he never had any luck. His prostate did him in.

Georges Larochelle had three passions — the encyclopedias he sold door-to-door, women, and my future. His first passion fed the second, which justified the third. The encyclopedias were the reason he found himself without my mother. He offered a free after-sale service that ruined his marriage.

"Larochelle," my mother said to him while scrambling the morning eggs, "I don't know why you feel obliged to explain the anatomy plates to all your lady customers."

She was exaggerating. My father did not offer the same service to all his customers, but if one of them bought all fourteen volumes of the Larousse Encyclopedia, he did feel an intellectual responsibility, as it were. Maman left. Papa, stuck in the house at night, read me pages out of his big books, and even gave me a magnifying glass so I could get a better look at the pictures. He worried about my education, signed me up with the good fathers, then found me brooding about what I was going to be: an engineer, lawyer, doctor, sociologist, dentist, pharmacist, notary ... I was eighteen.

"Join the Jesuits, Michel," he said, "You'll always get your bed and board, and if you jump the fence, the Virgin Mary won't ask for a divorce."

Maman went the distance. Legal proceedings, confrontations, witnesses, declaratory judgment, alimony collected by her lawyer, which bled our travelling salesman dry. Papa was finished. He didn't survive long enough to see me complete my novitiate. In accordance with his last wishes, I scattered his ashes in a field of thistles, "Beautiful flowers that can protect themselves." I've painted them on my coat of arms.

I joined the Jesuits, I studied theology and other futilities. Ignatius of Loyola provides the rule and the uniform, and we of the rank and file provide the conceit and ambition. I am a summa cum laude graduate of one of the universities of our Intelligence Branch, in Chicago. It should be understood that, while the Company works closely with people in Intelligence (as it's called in English), the Superior General of the Jesuits, who is in Rome, should not bear the brunt of blame for the escapades of some of his soldiers. I must stress that all Jesuit fathers are not spies just because they belong to an international congregation; the problem is the Company's penchant for secrecy of the kind cultivated by secret services. You never know whether this chemistry professor at our college in Tokyo, or that Latin teacher in Timbuktu, is working for the greater glory of God or the greater power of the West. These divided loyalties do add spice to the vocation. It's a simple matter: true Jesuits wear hair shirts to conquer their perverse impulses, and false Jesuits use their black robes to hide their lusts — which makes them all the worse, Papa would have said.

When I left university at the age of twenty-four, I took my mercenary vows: poverty, chastity, mendacity. They started me off with some delicate little jobs in Greece, where our archaeologists were being watched too closely by the authorities, then in Singapore, where the government was jeopardizing our imports of Cuban tobacco. I loved travelling, interminable meals taken in the company of aging fathers, theological problems raised by science, philosophical discussions, the practice of mental restriction, and the charm of mature women attracted by my cassock. An exquisite routine until this mission, which, for all my efforts, as I have said, has taken a turn as corrosive as sulphuric acid. Wealth, allurement, rebellion ...

When one has several university degrees and wears a cassock as uniform, one's most important tool for success is the art of accommodating truth. I learned this political skill very young while trying to mediate between my father and mother in their endless conjugal squabbles, redescribing reality until it pleased them in hues of fulgurating truth. I know there's an orphan's soul in me that longs to rescue every widow and is automatically the advocate of lost causes. I have never refused a job, and my superiors take advantage of my keen sense of duty. This is what has led me to retire from sight on the Avenue de l'Impératrice in Biarritz in this month of May, 1967.

This whole business began, you might say, last December 22 when the personal plane of the King of kings set down gently at Fiumicino airport. The Emperor of Ethiopia was arriving in Rome to seek help discreetly from the Catholic Church. There was of course no question of a personal meeting between the pope and the Lion of Juda, the two belonging to churches that had been separate for centuries, ever since a falling-out concerning the Holy Ghost: an ancient squabble over seating precedence at table for the persons of the Holy Trinity. Notwithstanding, the Roman Curia did not wish to miss an opportunity for rapprochement, because the cardinals, of course, have eaten ecumenism for breakfast since Roncalli called the Vatican Council together four years ago, and the time is ripe now, if ever, to buy old pectoral crosses set with rubies at bargain prices. The sovereign pontiff therefore delegated Monsignor Sambrini of the Holy Office, a wily diplomat and the Vatican's *chargé d'affaires* for Africa, to represent him. A Vatican Rolls Royce came to take the Emperor from the plane to a papal villa south of Rome, where His Majesty, over dinner, revealed the purpose of his unprecedented visit. While admiring the villa's cypresses and statues in the light of the setting sun, he congratulated himself on his strategy: he was outfoxing all the spies in his kingdom by requesting help from yesterday's invaders.

With a telex message the very next morning, Rome enquired of the Province of Canada as to the availability of a soldier of the Company of Jesus. The Emperor had already planned a trip to North America before springtime to seek technical aid from the Canadian and United States governments, who were promising to support his mission of educating the outrageously illiterate Abyssinian people. He would kill two birds with one stone and, during the trip, meet the Jesuit chosen for this new, special mission.

The Curia could hardly have been put on the spot at a worse time. For some months, recruits had been defrocking in droves and our ranks were being decimated by a lifestyle revolution. The faith had lost authority, and the hierarchies were being rendered voiceless, shaken by carnal chaos. Fruits of the earth perfumed the air. What was the Provincial superior to do? Turn to the ranks of the young, spot a heroic strain, a young Jesuit of both physical strength and moral courage. My early record was faultless, and I was approached. The Company's reputation was at stake; there was not a moment's hesitation on my part.

"Operation Rimbaud," announced the Provincial superior, who had always loved mystery, code names, passwords, Boy Scouts, adventure. Like all classical college students in Quebec, I knew the city of Harar through the biography of the poet Arthur Rimbaud, and I knew Arthur too, I told myself, but I really knew nothing about the faraway land of the Queen of Sheba. My paternal encyclopedia recalled emphatically that the Second World War had truly begun with the invasion of Abyssinia; that in 1936, the Emperor Hailé Selassie had come to Geneva to beseech the League of Nations to come to his aid, but in vain. The Western nations beat around the bush — Mussolini was one of theirs, the Negus a comic opera king. It was the British who helped reconquer Ethiopia, and the Emperor became a figurehead of freedom who believes, as my father believed, in education as the doorway to modernity. Destiny caused our paths to cross for sure, because what else could account for this meeting between a king and the son of a door-to-door salesman?

To emerge from the Middle Ages, Hailé Selassie had long put his hopes in a generation of girls and boys whom he had sent to study in foreign universities. But things had gone wrong. At our first private meeting, in a suite at the Windsor Hotel in Montreal, I found a pretty depressed head of state. The Lion of Juda, disheartened by ingratitude, seemed to have lost all confidence in humanity. "The very ones I have placed in the schools are openly preparing rebellion," he confided to me. He could count neither on the army nor the militia, for ambitious colonels had set up cells in both, and of course the clergy could not defend him. But what really got his goat was that the country people he had brought to the city one by one to be educated were now pretentious little bumpkins turned against him. That day, I can tell you, the Lion of Juda's mane was adroop, he was a picture of misery. He was seated in a blue velvet armchair, with his feet on a cushion so that his little legs would not dangle. His beard and moustache were meticulously trimmed, and his slightly balding pate was circled by a laurel-like wreath of salt-and-pepper hair. He wore a field marshal's uniform, while I had put on a brand new cassock and stood deferentially before him, as it behooved me in the circumstances.

The Negus spoke so softly one might suspect he was afraid the room was bugged, which was not impossible. "I know what's going to happen," he muttered, "they'll attempt a

putsch, assassinate or exile my sons, set up a puppet government, find a way to neutralize me; the army will take power
and the people will suffer." A prophet.

I was thinking to myself that he was talking to the wrong
person. He didn't need Jesuits, he needed the American army
or the CIA to deal with those nascent Marxist cells. But
he had been asking for trouble, too. Since his return to
government in Addis Ababa, he had been acting the sly dog,
playing the Americans against the Soviets, the British against
the French, allowing one country to open a clinic, another
to sell arms, this one to subsidize a high school, that one to
manage experimental farms. He thought he could guarantee
his independence by juggling the balance of influences. He
should have known that communists cheat at Monopoly.

Of course, Hailé Selassie himself was no lamb of God.
After the death of King Menelik, he had been grossly deceitful
in order to seize power. Did he remember the cruelty with
which he had captured the throne for himself? His cousin,
Princess Zauditu, was the rightful heiress, but for two years
she had been suffering from tuberculosis. Prince Selassie
was returning at the time from a period of study in Paris and
London. Flourishing his new-found knowledge, he recommended to the court physicians a treatment then in fashion
in the important centres of Europe, he said, giving as examples
the sanatoriums of Switzerland, to which tubercular patients
were flocking from the world over, seeking the fresh, salu-
brious air of the Alps.

Pulmonary ailments are treated in the mountains, the prince explained to Zauditu. Why not take advantage of Ethiopia's own sierras? He recommended that his ailing cousin take hot baths, after which, on nights when the moon was full, she should dry herself standing naked on the heights in the open air with her arms crossed over her breasts, face to the wind. Zauditu was not very sharp, and Selassie was already the king of foxes. Did he really believe so strongly in the healing power of pure air? This, in any event, is how the Ras Makonnen became the Negus Negushi, the King of kings, and his cousin a figure of legend.

I looked anxiously at the small, vexed potentate, wondering why the Company of Jesus had sent me to his side. This strange man, who once undoubtedly had irresistible charisma, looked, with his smooth, dark skin, like a figure from the yellowed pictures in my missal.

"I know," he added softly, "that Abyssinia even nowadays is a bagatelle in the eyes of your nations. But governments fall every day into the hands of the communists. I have warned the allies. They are still not hearing me."

"Westerners trust you, Your Majesty. You have been received in Washington."

"Trust without military support does not go very far," the Negus replied. "I envy the revolutionaries, who have found all the help they need."

"Your Majesty, how can I be of service?"

Would he ever get to the point, with his typically African

way of approaching the nub of a question a little bit at a time? I was thinking about launching appeals in neighbouring countries. We had Jesuits stationed in Egypt and others in Kenya. What if Gamal Abdel Nasser, one of the best students at our college in Cairo (back when King Farouk was exacting tribute in gold to match his weight) decided to help the Emperor? To all my suggestions, the Lion of Juda kept replying, "It's too late, too late ... that's not what I need, I have to be sure of staying above the fray ..."

I didn't know what else to suggest.

"Perhaps," I ventured, "you would like me to organize a press campaign in favour of your undertakings?"

The Emperor cut me short with his stare alone, his small head thrust forward, his dark eyes like burning coals in his emaciated face, his lips trembling as he searched for words to properly express his thoughts.

"Don't be naive! I have no time to waste with journalists ..."

I wasn't being naive, I was being careful. You can hide a lot under a cassock, a miscellany of weapons, machine guns, revolvers, knives, radios, cards you can lay down to win the game. But that day I couldn't hide anything from the Emperor. He had succeeded in making me feel sorry for him.

I said gravely, "Your Majesty, my superiors have ordered me to place myself at your disposal without restriction. With all due respect, that is what I am doing."

I saw a smile. I thought, a seasoned Jesuit would not have expressed himself better. Hailé Selassie will be my pope, my military and spiritual leader. I was pleased with myself. I expected him to hold out his arms to me. All he did was let out a hoarse cry that woke up two young chihuahuas, which came trotting over the Persian rug to him and laid their muzzles on the cushion at his feet, emitting plaintive yowls. Was I supposed to do likewise? Does an emperor expect that degree of submission? I had no desire to get down on all fours and bark!

The Negus stroked his pups as he looked at me, then said softly and soberly, "There is a legend people believe, which does not offend me and I know is not a figment of my imagination, but history. Listen to me carefully: I, Monsieur Larochelle, am the custodian of the Tablets of the Law. You have heard of them?"

He looked at me defiantly. A Jesuit could well understand what he was talking about, and even more, a Québécois suckled at the biblical nipple.

My neurons and synapses raced back over time, the Old Testament, those encyclopedias; I was overcome by a rush of gratitude to my father.

"In truth, Your Majesty, I recall that Moses, when guiding the tribe of Israel, received the Tablets of Judaic Law from the very hands of God."

"Just so, Monsieur Larochelle. While the Israelites were allowing themselves to be enticed by Satan and his idols, Moses, having led his people out of Egypt, spent days and nights on Mount Sinai, where he received from God the Torah and its Commandments."

"And you ..."

"Those stones are today in my possession. They are my strength and my power, they must absolutely not fall into impious hands."

So this was what our conversation was about. Did he really believe this claptrap? Through the window behind him, I could see a sunny Montreal. Leafless maple trees, the automatic parking garage on Stanley Street where an elevator lifted cars eight floors, a billboard advertising Players' cigarettes, electric wires strung from pole to pole, criss-crossing the landscape. And before me, a little man with two ridiculous little dogs at his feet, telling me calmly that he was the possessor of Moses's Tablets of the Law. Did he carry them around in his luggage? Was I supposed to believe in them, too? Eternal God! God Most High! If the old fellow was telling me he believed in the Tablets, who was I to contradict him? Besides, I remembered a lesson taught me by my teacher in Chicago: always leave the window open a crack for the unimaginable. In my trade, you mustn't ever swear by anything, or brush off all possibility of magic.

"You can't keep putting your finger in Jesus's wounds," said Father Rodriguez, who was my guardian angel during the Exercises prescribed by Saint Ignatius, and who subsequently became my best friend. "After sophistry, the danger awaiting us is sterility," he added, observing that despite their literature courses, our colleges produced few poets. "Our clients are often motivated by curious passions that we must adapt to." He was speaking with the voice of experience. I would adapt.

The Emperor leapt from his chair like a boy jumping out of bed. "I have asked your superiors to second you to my service," he said in a low voice with a slight London accent, "but before we reach an agreement, I want to ask you a question ..." He walked to and fro, making me giddy with his pacing. Then he came and planted himself in front of me, his head level with my chest. Behind him, the chihuahuas began to yap uncontrollably.

"If I put the Tablets of the Law in your care, what would you do?"

Now I saw that I was cornered, like Moses, and like him as well, no doubt, I suddenly felt very much alone in the world. The Tablets of the Law in the hands of an agnostic Jesuit, baptized in the chapel of Notre-Dame Hospital, according to the rites of the Roman Catholic Church, whether I liked it or not! Really! Outrageous! An awesome idea! I didn't believe in God, but the thought that he could have dictated whatever he wanted didn't seem so outlandish. And then, maybe once upon a time God did exist. After all, they'd been trumpeting his death for over a hundred years ... What was written on those ancient tablets? The Ten Commandments. I remembered the first: "Thou shalt have no other gods before me." Of course. It was in his own interest.

"Your Majesty, you are aware that I am associated with the Church of Rome ..."

"And I with the Church of Alexandria. These are only administrative questions; we are both Christians, Monsieur Larochelle. The Amharas, who are my ancestors, converted to Christianity several centuries ago, and the Tablets of the Law have been located in our Empire since the destruction of the Temple of Jerusalem. They were brought by caravan to the coast of Egypt, and there placed on barges that carried them up the Bahr-el-Azrak, the Blue Nile, to Khartoum, to where our kingdom extended at the time, before the Muslim invasions. It is the tablets that have enabled us to stand firm to this day against the sons of Muhammed. What do you think about this?"

Churchill, Roosevelt, de Gaulle, Nehru, Mao, Hailé Selassie, the faces of these giants sprang to my mind — I had been summoned by History. What would I do? As a child, I had learned to chew a matter over well in my mind before speaking, the better to dress the truth.

"You will allow me to think about what I would do, Your Majesty," I replied. "I will not improvise on a matter of this importance. I promise you on my honour to protect them, take the greatest care of them, keep them in a Christian country, but I cannot decently offer you a complete and adequate answer now."

The little man with the proud head of hair looked at me with satisfaction, then held out his left hand. On it glittered a gold ring set with a sapphire, and on this ring I laid my lips to seal our agreement.

"Monsieur Larochelle, I do not think you will have too much trouble accomplishing your mission," he said as he dismissed me.

2

BIARRITZ IS SITUATED ON A magnificent promontory and is a former fishing port transformed into an artificial locality where hotels, concrete, restaurants, and expensive shop-windows have taken over all available space. Retirees dressed in white or sky blue straggle about on the sidewalks waiting for the next meal or the time to arrive for cocktails by the pool.

To keep in shape, I jog several kilometres a day from the hotel's pathways to the casino, usually by way of the beach. We are far from unspoiled nature here, and the streets I take in the direction of the Pyrenees are scattered with opulent villas that would plant the seeds of revolution in any African.

But back to the events that brought me here.

It hadn't taken me long to organize myself and leave for Addis Ababa. The reservations had been made by Rome in the name of Monsieur Michel Larochelle, engineer, without mention of any religious connection. This was my first trip to Africa and I had no intention of posing as one of the bona fide missionaries. I would be a businessman whose purpose was to sell radio-telephone installations. I was arriving with my catalogues, my backpack, and my light suit made of Tergal polyester the colour of wet sand, with shirt collar open, and eyes, too.

The Ethiopian Airlines plane, flown by former TWA pilots, Americans past their glory days, put down nonchalantly on tarmac as potholed and weed-strewn as a country road. At the end of the runway, the plane's four propellers each coughed two or three times and then dozed off as if exhausted.

I had slept during the last hours of the trip, unsuccessfully groping for images of a childhood buried in the furthest recesses of my unconscious. Did I even have a childhood, in fact? It seems I was one of those children who grow up before their time, more mature than my parents, whose childish behaviour I would watch for anxiously. I loved them both. Papa was an ocean of knowledge, Maman a haven of safety. Why couldn't they get along? Who were those ladies that kept Papa away from home? Maman was in the movies, wasn't she, on the screen, like Catherine Deneuve? I was so serious, so studious, so worried all the time, that no present-day adventure could make up for the carefree hours lost to me while I held my progenitors by the hand. I had let the enjoyment of Meccano and collecting baseball cards pass me by. It was a bit late now in any case to start having childhood pleasures again.

In the distance, a gaily garbed crowd pressed against the high metal fence around the airport, holding black umbrellas to the sun. From above, Addis Ababa looked like a white metal lake dotted with islets of eucalyptus growing in the greatest disorder. At ground level, the city was no more than a huge, semi-abandoned worksite scattered about a sparse forest, all of it horizontally streaked with blue haze. Plumes of smoke rose from small chimneyless huts. I watched two ragged workmen push a rusty set of stairs toward us. It wobbled on its three wheels. The American pilots got off first, then the passengers, foreigners mostly, merchants, engineers, and teachers, who set off for the customs house built of cement blocks with a corrugated tin roof held down by stones. Were the locals afraid it might fly away?

"*Corcoro*," said my neighbour in the queue that had formed at the customs-house door. "That," he added, "is what corrugated iron is called in this country. And in the morning on the corcoro, cocks do their cock-a-doodle-doo." Did he expect me to bust a gut? He was an odd sight, with his green checkered vest and his red hair, as if he was stepping out of a movie in Technicolor. "What have you come to this godforsaken country for?" Was he naturally curious or just a natural-born pain in the butt?

"How about you?" I asked warily.

John Dougherty was a cattle-raising specialist arriving from Dakota. He was an old hand at international missions, worked for the Food and Agriculture Organization. A hick.

We were moving at a snail's pace in line, which gave us time to exchange business cards. He was on his third mission in the country. The great plains could feed a lot more mouths than people thought, he insisted, if only they were farmed sensibly.

"What a coincidence," I said, "the American government has given us an exploratory contract. I've come bearing a message of hope." And I smiled my broadest smile. The hick looked at me incredulously. I continued: "We intend to set up a radio-meteorological network to help Ethiopian farmers. I represent Metra, a Canadian subsidiary that manufactures certain elements of the network, equipment that's on the technological cutting edge."

"A lot of good it'll do them," the man replied, scratching his back as though a swarm of fleas had invaded it, which was not unlikely. "The problem for native farmers is drought, it's true, but I don't see how a network of precise forecasting is going to be any use to them."

"Governments follow strange fancies sometimes, you know. The government of the United States has decided to make this gift to the Emperor, who visited the country recently."

"Then it's the army that's going to use your communications network!" Dougherty retorted with a disdainful pout.

Before I could reply, I found myself facing a customs officer in a brass-buttoned khaki uniform, a woollen beret on his noggin, who, with an air of distrust, had decided to inspect all the seams of my bag after emptying it on the table in front of him. My neighbour had forgotten me and was attending to his own business. To each his own threshold of privacy, and I loathed seeing my socks, toilet articles, undershirts, and briefs displayed in public. I was in a foul mood, but the uniformed lout, oblivious to that, was visibly taken by my Minolta, an old but exceptionally fine camera complete with perfect lenses, of which I was particularly fond.

"Do you have a permit?"

He wished to keep the camera for further verification and would return it to me, he said, the following day. In these parts, I had been warned, following days have the colour of eternity. I had taken pains for there to be nothing official about my arrival and already I was having to change my plans. I was very angry, almost dancing with rage — not like me at all — when I asked to see the customs supervisor immed- iately and, in the grubby little office where he was dozing behind a forest of official stamps, placed under his nose the diplomatic passport adorned with a visa signed by the Minister of the Interior, which had been delivered to me on my departure from Montreal.

The customs supervisor jumped to his feet. Cooing like a mating pigeon, he wanted to apologize. His employee would be disciplined for his zeal, I could count on it, all I needed to do now was pick up a few thalers at the exchange wicket for the tip. I recovered my bag, my Minolta, my personal articles in disarray, thanked the supervisor grumpily, then found myself in the company of Mr. Dougherty, who offered to share a taxi with me.

The road from the airport to the city was long enough, but the overflows of local traffic, gharries, Vespas, heavy trucks, horses, and beat-up or burned-out jalopies made it even longer.

Was the doughty Dougherty my guardian angel? Was it his job to protect me? He prattled away like a journalist, called my attention to the aberrations of all that traffic on such a narrow highway and pointed out certain buildings we passed, like a government ministry and the English hospital, pronouncing the local language so badly I couldn't grasp a thing of what he was showing me.

Gradually, there were more large buildings and denser crowds; the taxi was moving at a snail's pace before being forced to stop completely. We were approaching the entrance to the main marketplace (the *mercato*, Dougherty told me), where a pickup truck had knocked over a cyclist. Or was it a donkey that had planted itself crosswise to the road?

"You'll learn to have patience in this country. You'll find out what your better attributes are. The place will forge your character for sure."

Children and cripples surrounded the immobilized taxi, whimpering and pleading for charity, and holding out a hand or stump, their eyes covered with flies, which they kept waving away with little effect.

"First test," Dougherty said to me coldly, "either you hand out what money you've got or you pretend you don't care. In the first case, you'll attract thousands of beggars and we'll never get away from here, in the second, you'll have to admit that the injustice is gross and these human beings would have every reason in the world to tear out your eyes along with your privileges."

The taxi driver turned around. Clearly, he understood English.

"Don't forget to keep enough money to pay the fare," he cut in with a chuckle.

I rolled up the car window to put a necessary distance between me and a leprous mother with her baby in rags. Lessons in charity were not due to a member of the Company of Jesus, I thought to myself, and I couldn't risk compromising my mission by staging on a cheap Good Samaritan show.

There were more and more cripples, there were dozens of them begging alms from us when at last the taxi began to move; two policemen shooed away the crowd and the car was able to drive into the city centre.

I asked Dougherty what attracted him to this country and why he came back so often.

"The Middle Ages present everywhere," he said, "the impression of travelling in time, of going back to the birth of our culture." Then he showed me a small, finely chased silver cross that he kept under his shirt. "They're still in the age of miracles here. It's a harsh country, but it's the real thing."

"Money, little money please." A Babel of languages soli-
cited charity before the tall doors of the Imperial Ghion. A
legless fellow was dragging himself, his hands on wooden
blocks, along the ground. It was heartbreaking. I followed
Dougherty as he passed with his head high, pretending not
to care.

The Ghion is a luxury hotel where foreign journalists and
international government officials like Dougherty take shelter.
I would have preferred to stay somewhere else, of course,
so I could have more elbow room, but the reservation had
been made by the ministry. I registered, said goodbye to my
taxi-mate, and followed the bellhop, who led me across a
pink marble lobby and into an elevator hidden behind some
tropical ferns.

It was only when I was in my room and after taking a long,
lukewarm shower that I realized why I had been feeling slightly
depressed since the landing at the airport. An advertising
folder reminded visitors that Addis Ababa was a young capital
city built at an altitude of nearly three thousand metres. I was
short of oxygen! A bagatelle in a caper like this, I told myself.

Through the window, I saw below me horses pulling carts
heavily loaded with lumber, a deserted parking lot, a garden
being watered by automatic sprinklers, and hardly any people
walking around. No one could realize what anxiety was gradually taking hold of me. Rooting out intelligence, uncovering
plots, identifying a murderer, that was always okay, but this
time I was being asked to transgress too many interdicts. The

Law of Moses applied beyond the borders of the kingdom, the tablets belonged to the human race, certainly not to the king. Did they know in Rome what I was getting myself into?

I lay down on the still-made bed and closed my eyes. I have been uneasy by nature all my life. An anxious man, for all my connections and experience. My mother, when she was pregnant with me, often went to the movies, she loved to go and see melodramas and action films, so I would have reels of film in my head turning in all directions. I drifted into a half-sleep.

What was I going to do with the tablets if I did manage to make off with them? I had turned the question over in my head seven thousand times without finding an answer. Had they counted on my age and inexperience when they chose me for this mission? I would have liked to consult Father Rodriguez, s.j., my teacher and friend, but I had not been able to obtain any useful information on his whereabouts before this trip, either from Washington or from Rome.

He had left Cairo without leaving an address, I had been told, in the company of a belly dancer famous throughout the Middle East. It seemed so much like an oriental fairy tale, the newspapers all gave their first pages to the couple on the run. The rector of the Jesuit College taking off with a luscious princess out of the *Thousand and One Nights*! The cartoonists portrayed him as a grand vizier, a woman whose ample endowments bespoke a Persian goddess at his feet. I couldn't believe it. Still, it would serve nothing to set the

church-circuit jungle-drums beating; not a single father of
the Company of Jesus would know how to find the renegade.
I was alone in the world while Father Rodriguez was whirling in the arms of a dancer! I fell sound asleep.

I dreamed that night that Dougherty and I had lashed the
tablets to the backs of very tall camels and were crossing
granite dunes by moonlight. The sacred stones were sparkling in the desert night. The American was on foot, wearing
a diving suit, and his flippers were leaving tracks that any good
hunter would be able to follow with ease. We were taking the
tablets to Rome to hide them under the Holy Father's canopy
bed. The reels kept turning and then there was a fade-out to
black and finally I could fall back into a restorative sleep.

When I woke in the early morning, on the twelfth floor of
the Imperial Ghion, in a big bed like those found in all the
Hiltons on earth, I felt reinvigorated and resolute. I believed
in my lucky star. I had found a solution. I had convinced
myself to take the Tablets of the Law first to Europe, where
I wanted to have them examined by experts in spite of all.
You don't get to put an artifact of this quality under the
microscope every day. I wanted to take photos of them, X-ray
them, evaluate their age, compare their writing. I needed a
laboratory. A bad habit of mine, this: I was busy conducting
expert examinations even before beginning my research.
It's a characteristic I've inherited from my father, I think,
this strange urge to have finished even before having begun.

A kind of anxiety, perhaps. But at least I can perform. I'm an entrepreneur in my fashion.

I was thinking about this again not long ago as I gazed out at the sea off Biarritz, buttered my toast, poured hot Jamaican coffee into my cup, and wiped my lips on the fine linen napkin embroidered with Eugénie's coat of arms. The circular dining room was almost empty and my eyes drifted from the silverware to the multicoloured, carefully arranged bouquets of flowers on the little pedestal tables. A small sign at the entrance announced the noon-hour banquet of the Basque Association of Ferrari Owners (Bayonne-Biarritz Section), who were gathering for their annual meeting. I thought to myself: what if I bought myself one, providing my plan works. The hotel parking lot looked like the shop windows of the Champs-Élysées, with red and chrome Ferraris shining in the sun, sparkling, tops up, golf clubs wedged behind black leather seats. To one of the owners who had a mug like a grocer's, I casually remarked, "They're really fine sculptures." His sole response was a haughty look down his nose. One day, my friend, I flung at him in my imagination, you'll find out what I'm really worth. But over a stupid matter of wounded pride, this was not the moment to yield to impatience, to play the offended Jesuits tune, not before pulling off Operation Tablets of God.

The countdown begins this morning. A week from now, my general in Rome will receive an envelope he is supposed to take to His Holiness. If all goes well, I shall be not only a Ferrari owner, but free of want for the rest of time. I shall become vain, I sense; I'll have to watch myself, it's my Achilles heel. I sent my two cassocks with their sashes to be pressed. The chambermaid couldn't resist when she brought them back. Ancillary *amours* are incredibly sweet. When I quit these premises, I shall leave my clerical clothing in the enormous walk-in closet as theatrical costumes that may be venerated by rising generations of Jesuits.

3

AT NINE O'CLOCK THE MORNING after my arrival, the King of kings's automobile came to pick me up to take me from the Ghion to the imperial palace. Emperors don't do things by halves. It was an immensely long Mercedes and I sat on the gently crinkled leather of the back seat, protected by tinted windows, and this time a good distance from pedestrians and beggars. Some individuals even dropped to their knees as we went by. I blessed them as I had seen bishops do. The city was swarming with people and full of life beneath a bright sun. Didn't it ever rain in this country?

The Negus had insisted that I come alone, which hardly conforms with the rules of our congregation, Jesuits always travelling in threes, be it in China or India. This way there is always a chaperone and opportunities for sinning are decreased. Better still, the trio is often composed of a man of letters, a scientist, and a political con man. The first two are there to impress and the third negotiates.

I didn't like taking on these responsibilities without support, but the Negus had promised me two local assistants in whom, he said, I could have total confidence. My cover was acceptable: a radio-telephone specialist with Metra, associated with Point Four, the American international aid program.

The Emperor had decided to grant me a morning audience, after receiving the usual representations from the clergy and village chiefs in the crowded great hall of the Ghebbi, along with reports from his ministers, and complaints from inhabitants of Addis Ababa who distrusted their mayor. A fine program, always exhausting, but one that enabled the head of state to know all. I was moved to see the Negus again. He would launch a new case with a cock of his chin, ask few questions, and render justice in the manner of his ancestor, Solomon — who had known the Queen of Sheba, who had come from black Abyssinia to Israel and seduced the King of the Hebrews.

I was contemplating the sense of history and thinking again of Dougherty. He was right, the Middle Ages were palpable here, all the way from the far corners of this damp hall, where the very stones were imbibed with the smell of the *berbere*, the red pepper with which all the indigenous cuisine is spiced. From under their white *shammas*, toga-like garments that one might imagine in Rome or Athens, some of the village chiefs emitted mingled smells of pepper and rancid butter. A delight for the eyes and the nose as well, aromas better than Givenchy's perfumes.

Did the Empress perfume her person? I caught myself wondering this as I scrutinized an immense painting in which Her Majesty, the Menen, was shown seated, a slight zen smile on her large, vacuous face. In perspective, she appeared to be six times the size of her husband, and her young children, seated around her, all looked more like her than like the Emperor: the same carp-like jowls, the same drooping shoulders, the same Byzantine eyes habitually painted by Afework Tekle, the court artist whose canvases mostly tended to recall El Greco, with his spindly figures seen through mysterious mists. A number of his paintings graced the walls of the Ghebbi, no doubt a source of endless pleasure to the bearded and beribboned priests hovering before His Majesty's throne. The queen, a Galla princess at the time, had accepted a political marriage. It was probably not a superlative love match for the royal couple; he as slender as a cheetah, she more like a hippopotamus. For the past five years in any event, the Emperor had been a widower; the Menen's heart had abdicated, owing to her corpulence.

The ceremony dragged on without any indication of rising impatience, and time sifted away slowly as if in a huge hourglass. To amuse myself, I counted the gold filaments in a princess's robe and the spiderweb filaments hanging from the tops of stone columns.

In my pocket, I had a list of all the good fathers from Canada and the United States scattered around the world. There were some behind the iron curtain, in Prague and Moscow, as well as in the Amazon forests, where they were preaching the Gospel to the natives, and in Buenos Aires, where they were advising the president. We could count on the Jesuit network to identify and target the elites in developing countries, of which Ethiopia was one, where, dressed in lay clothes, we ran the only college of higher learning in Addis Ababa. I promised myself I would make contact with my brethren as soon as possible; I didn't want to involve them in my mission, but I should be able to approach them for an interpreter, refuge, perhaps money.

I didn't really like the idea of finding myself isolated like a lone duck at the beginning of hunting season. I kept scanning the crowd seated at the feet of the princes for a familiar face, or a sign. Who were my companions on the job going to be? The men all bore themselves proudly, the women were gentle-eyed. Most belonged to the same tribe as the Negus, with slim noses, crinkly hair, and skin of a delicate brown; other Ethiopians were easily distinguishable in the crowd, blacker, stockier. Then, near the main door, I saw Dougherty, who was craning his neck. I must admit that, with relief, I felt both watched and less alone.

A majordomo came and plucked at my sleeve. It was my turn to approach the Lion of Judah. I did as I had seen others do, walking with small steps on the carpet leading to the feet of the Emperor, my body respectfully bent forward a little, my hands on the side seams of my pants. When I arrived at the steps of the podium, I bowed very low, but without putting a knee to the ground like the natives. A Jesuit bends but does not humble himself.

"Welcome to our kingdom!" the Emperor declared vivaciously. "Word of your competency has echoed all the way to our high plateaus. Your knowledge of radio-telephone technology is going to be of great value to us. We thank you for coming to be among us." I looked at the Negus as he lied with aplomb, wondering if I should reply, but His Majesty continued: "Shortly, Monsieur Larochelle, you will dine with us and our minister responsible for agricultural affairs. We shall also talk about proposals from the World Bank." Then, to show he knew what was going on, he added: "An envoy from the FAO, Mr. Dougherty, whom you have met, I believe, wants to help us develop the growing of coffee. We are very proud of our coffee; it grows wild in our mountains and our coffee beans are the best in the world."

The crowd, which had been silent till then, began to applaud thunderously. I was just a mite disappointed when I realized that the tribute was not addressed to me (that little sin of vanity) but to the coffee gatherers. A liveried chamberlain straight out of an illustration from a Jules Verne novel came forward to offer me, on a silver tray suspended from three delicate chains, a demitasse of steaming coffee. The Emperor, who had already been served, lifted his own miniature cup toward me, his little finger curled like a cock's spur, and I drank the magic potion with delight, thanking him for his thoughtfulness.

In the seconds that followed, I saw the Emperor jump to his feet and the natives bow to the ground, even the high dignitaries of the clergy, as the diminutive king left, to the accompaniment of strident ululations from the women, a sound that became unbearable inside the hall. Everyone went out through a sculptured door into the gardens where a tent had been set up for the banquet.

Dougherty made his way up beside me.

"So we're partners, then?" I suggested to him, but he seemed not to understand my question and just asked if I had brought my knife.

"I'm not Caligula," I replied. "Why would I have a knife?"

"In the Middle Ages, one never leaves home without one's dagger," said Dougherty, who seemed to be as entertained as at the theatre.

The protocol chief, a tall, thin man who might have stepped out of a Giacometti exhibition, seated me to the right of the Negus. The Minister of Agriculture, dressed in a dark, three-piece western suit over which he had thrown his shamma, came and sat at my right. The King of kings was dining on his throne while we were seated at a lower level at a long table, elbow to elbow, with no one facing us. Dougherty, beside the minister, and a dozen other diners could thus exchange confidences out of the corners of their mouths without fearing indiscreet ears. The other guests were seated in circles under the tent.

The Emperor leaned toward me and said sarcastically, "My minister only understands English."

I sensed that I ought not reply.

"Monsieur Larochelle," he pursued, "you are under sentence to accomplish your mission. The continued existence of the kingdom is in your hands. At ten o'clock tonight, in the bar at the Ghion, you will meet your associates. You can count on them, they are totally devoted. You will also consult Mr. Dougherty, who may be helpful in matters of geography, but be warned, he knows nothing of our plan. He's a Protestant, a technician, and he talks three times a day with Washington. If you have logistical problems, he may also be useful to you. Bon appétit!"

A procession of servers arrived, two by two, some bearing woven baskets, others soup tureens, and the last, great silver dishes filled with raw, bleeding meat. Was it beef or prisoner? The Minister of Agriculture gracefully lifted the cover of a basket and took out some cold, soft, pancake-type bread, which he tore into strips and placed in Dougherty's plate and mine.

"*Injera*," he said, then gestured for the soup tureen to be proffered; its bright red contents looked like a witch's brew; "*wat*," he added, and using a knife he had produced from under his jacket, he speared pieces of meat, which he divided between the American and me.

There was no fork or other utensil, no vegetables, no millet; a diner took a chunk of raw meat between his teeth, slashed a piece off it from beneath with his knife — without damaging his nose — spat the flesh into a piece of pancake, dipped it all in the spicy soup, then ate it with expressions of blissful enjoyment. The berbere, one might say, cooked the meat on contact. Hugely amused at my expense, Dougherty handed me a Swiss knife that he had in his pocket. I set about eating like everyone else; a Jesuit adapts to any culture, even though he must suffer a thousand deaths the next day.

Between two mouthfuls, the minister asked me to explain the Metra system that the Americans intended to give the country. I gave a brilliant demonstration of the benefits of meteorological prediction and the fact that in case of catastrophe or other necessity the radio network would become an essential instrument of civil protection. Dougherty did not contradict me, on the contrary, and added four million dollars American in subsidies. The minister was delighted, but I felt humiliated by the FAO barbarian who had lent me his knife. Henceforth, I would make enquiries about ways and customs before letting myself look like a fool.

When the Negus rose and all the diners prepared to leave the tent, the minister did us the signal honour, Dougherty and me, of escorting us to the palace gates, from where we could see, in the middle of the traffic circle, four caged imperial lions, roaring with pleasure while hungrily tearing apart whole quarters of calves, gazelles, or young goats.

"Like masters, like servants," Dougherty remarked to me guardedly as he led me to a Vespa serving as a taxi. The little motor scooter took us, backfiring, from the park of Arat Kilo to downtown, while I, squeezed into the back seat, undertook to question the FAO envoy, who was voluble.

He was a fiftyish man, married, he told me, but in the process of separating from a wife who did not want to leave the suburbs of Cincinnati. Yes, he admitted, he had been pressed into service by the CIA, at the request of the Emperor, to make sure I would fit into the landscape as well as possible. Which reminded me to give him back his Swiss knife, thanking him heartily for playing Scout leader. He was leaving the next day for Nairobi and insisted that I know who I was up against. He told me that the communists had been accumulating arms and munitions for a year and a half and stashing them in different churches in the capital. The caravans left the Red Sea, crossed through Somalia, and took a week to reach the caches of the revolutionary party, which was led by young officers of the imperial guard. Dougherty believed an attack to be imminent, rumours of a putsch were already circulating at the mercato.

"But how can these caravans travel halfway across Ethiopia without being discovered?"

The Vespa was shaking us like a pair of dice and the American was shouting in my ear to be heard above the sound of the two-stroke engine, which the driver was making buzz like a bumblebee around a flower.

"The strategy is to slowly stifle the capital. The provincial governors have their palms greased every time a caravan passes. The Emperor doesn't have a chance to turn things around. Your mission is to help him leave the country, I suppose. I have some ideas about that, we can talk about it at the hotel."

Emptying a bottle of Chivas Regal as he paced back and forth in the room, Dougherty gave me a passionate lecture on how to extricate the Emperor from the hornet's nest. He had envisioned an escape in stages, and the plan he described seemed to me ideal for transporting the Tablets of the Law. I was not going to let him know what mission I had been given, but details of steps to be taken, names of possible accomplices, available caches, available cash, all this was going to be useful and his counsel was stored away in the left corner of my brain. We agreed to meet again three weeks later; I preferred knowing he'd be at a precise location, rather than keep wondering if he was following me like my shadow. I chose Marseille, where we could hide the Negus if need be, I allowed him to understand.

When Dougherty left my room, he stank of whisky and cigarette smoke. I closed the door behind him and went out onto the little balcony to breathe the fresh air, my hands in my pockets. The altitude was giving me a strange illusion of power, as if the universe were at my feet. Temptation in the desert. Satan was prowling, perhaps. The sounds of the city rose to my ears, mingling in the wind with the scent borne from the eucalyptus trees. I was beginning to contemplate eternity when a concert of car horns from the direction of the cathedral proclaimed the beginning of a nighttime celebration. I had an appointment in the Ghion bar on the penthouse floor, and this is where I now went, as the Emperor had asked me to.

The room was striking, illuminated from below, the translucent floor lighting the space as if one were imagining the planet Mars, everything bathed in a phosphorescent glow. As customers crossed the room from the elevator, each one would cast shadows on the ceiling, giving the place a ghost-haunted air. Deep leather chairs opened their arms to drinkers, whose reassuring presence one detected from the glow of their cigarettes. I headed for a stool at the end of the counter near the cash register and ordered my favourite drink, a Bloody Mary, because, as is known, the Virgin is the mascot of the Company of Jesus. The barman replaced the Tabasco sauce with berbere, but could I have decently hoped otherwise? A thousand deaths, I thought, telling myself that I would be spending the night with my posterior in the bathtub, trying to extinguish the flames of hellfire.

All barmen at great hotels are the same. Here, at the Hôtel du Palais in Biarritz, there's a Catalan, a bald and rather pleasant fellow who makes cocktails but doesn't speak to you unless you insist. The Amhara who made my Bloody Mary was no more talkative. Is this a directive in these palatial establishments? And what kind of people can enjoy these premises where the corridors are cluttered with show windows full of jewellery by Cartier, watches by Jaeger-LeCoultre, and silk prayer rugs?

"Have you seen customers buy these things?" I asked the Catalan, who answered a bit coolly that, yes indeed, gentlemen motivated by passion sometimes gave diamonds and pearl necklaces to their wives to celebrate their good luck on returning from the casino. Others, this very night, in this very place, had discussed the purchase of two purebred Arabian horses; one of the customers, an Italian, recited a poem aloud while the other was writing a cheque in the millions.

"An ode to the equine race?" I asked, and the barman, after assuring himself that we were alone, repeated for me what the Italian had recited, and of which I, astonished, took careful note:

Hot blood pulsing in exceptionally fine tissues; generosity at the brink of overflow, at the brink of incomprehension; a desire to be loved at the brink of insufferable jealousy, ancestral habitation of the nomadic life with man, at the brink of intelligence, the feline beauty, at times equivocal, of a stallion at the brink of femininity ...

His voice was warm and melodic. What erudition! This is what sets apart a barman at a four-star from one at a corner tavern who only hears the acid confidences of cuckolded husbands.

This poem to Arabian horses might have applied to the couple who approached me in the semi-darkness of the bar. She was muscular and feline, while he looked like a clone of His Majesty in a taller and younger version. Both, impeccably dressed in black under fine, glistening white shammas, introduced themselves.

"Véronik."

"Tafari. You were expecting us?"

And they invited me to follow them to an isolated table, where we sat on a banquette covered in leopard skin. My glass had followed and had multiplied by three.

The young woman and the boy were on drawing-room behaviour, deferent and smiling. All three of us were there by requisition — there was a distance between us that had to be overcome. I was quite obviously the outsider, it was up to me to win their confidence.

"To your health!" I said brightly, raising my glass.

Tafari, as he had introduced himself, drank a mouthful of his Bloody Mary and added: "I've always believed that drinking the same drinks makes it easier to come to meetings of minds."

The young woman sipped several times at her vodka and then said, laughing: "You don't look at all like a Jesuit father!"

"Ah," I said, "so you can tell a man's a Jesuit when you see him?"

"Shiny cassock, hair plastered down, dandruff on his shoulders, aquiline nose, an inspired air about him ..."

"Delighted to know I don't look like that caricature!" I told her, making a face.

"Véronik was teasing," Tafari put in. "Don't take it wrong."

"And you," I rejoined, "you're the spitting image of the King of kings."

"Yet I'm not even a prince," Tafari replied. "My sister Véronik and I are natural children of His Majesty. Don't be surprised that I admit being a bastard, the whole court knows it but nobody pays any attention to that anymore."

"You'll excuse me for the ridiculous description ..." Véronik hastened to add. "That's what they used to say at the school in Switzerland where I studied. They were anticlerical there ..."

"You studied in Switzerland ..."

"The Emperor has cared for us since we were born," Véronik continued, "and he has continued to do so in spite of our mother's marriage to a rich Armenian industrialist here in the capital. We don't live with him anymore, but we go with him on certain trips abroad. Tafari and I admire him hugely."

"His determination to transform the country runs counter to the selfishness of landowners and the interests of certain ministers," Tafari interjected. "But until last year we had reason to think he was going to win his gamble, he has put so much effort and money into it."

"I don't think the Emperor's intentions can be doubted," I agreed quickly.

"It's his methods that weren't perhaps the right ones," Tafari said. "And then, time has played against him." Emptying his glass, he added, "But we aren't here to talk about the politics of the kingdom. Has your stay begun well?"

I noted for my own purposes that both of them remained critical of royal undertakings. Then I explained briefly that Dougherty, whom I had just left, had outlined the situation for me.

"He worried me at first. I didn't know where to fit him in the picture. He's a CIA agent, of course."

They were aware of that.

How old might they be? They seemed a little younger than I, Véronik around thirty, her brother two or three years younger, yet everything about Tafari, his gestures, his eyes, even his voice, revealed an above-average maturity and knack for authority. I put down my glass and asked: "And our plans?"

Tafari handed me a sheet of paper folded in four on which he had drawn a cube and specifications.

"Tomorrow morning," he said, "would you please order two wooden crates to be built with these dimensions. In one we will transport the tablets, the other will enable us to dispose of the old Abouna and his servant. You should understand that this patriarch never leaves the sacred room where the stones are preserved. He lives there day and night, accompanied by an armed guard who is responsible both for protecting his master and for preventing him from leaving. We're in a delicate situation here."

"The air in the room is almost unbreathable," Véronik continued, "the incense that has been burning there for centuries has so impregnated the hangings, the canopies, and the altar. The old man hasn't seen the light of day for eight months; he only goes outside, with the Tablets of the Law, once a year for the procession of the Meskal. Then he goes back to the cave."

"You've seen and touched these stones? Are they heavy? How big are they?" I was talking to Tafari.

"A strong man can carry them one by one. There are two. I don't even know if we have the authentic tablets there or copies, but for the monks of the monastery there's no doubt, or for the people, either — they're by the hand of Moses."

"I thought they were by the very hand of God!" Or had I misread my Bible?

"You should be ashamed, Father Larochelle! Saint Ignatius will be turning over in his vault ..."

I raised my hand to silence Véronik.

"Stop, I beg you! I don't want to hear any more allusions to my religious status. This is a question for debate between the Creator and me."

Véronik shrugged her shoulders as she persisted: "But

the Emperor told us that you belonged to the Company of Jesus."

"All right, that's so. But like the two of you, I'm a bastard. My boss is in Rome, I belong to the Company, but apart from that I freelance, understand?"

"Jesuit and mercenary?" she said.

"Or the other way round. I'd rather we put our allegiances aside and concentrate on our operation."

"Still," Tafari cut in, settling down in his armchair, "you ought to know that the first tablets were by the hand of God, sure enough, but the day Moses came down from the mountain and found his people kneeling before a golden calf, he flew into a terrible rage and threw the tablets on the ground; they broke, he had to begin again from zero."

Véronik lit a cigarette with a sly smile.

"And God, to teach him a lesson, made Moses take the stylet and himself engrave the Ten Commandments, *Monsieur* Larochelle."

"And because this was long before Xerox, here we are with the two original copies. Numbered, so to speak ..."

Tafari then became more serious. "I can assure you, *Hailé Selassie mutt*, I swear it by Hailé Selassie, that they have extraordinary properties, if not miraculous. But more important, these tablets are still today the foundation of Western morality."

The Emperor's son had put his finger on the key: of all the sacred objects venerated throughout the centuries, the

Tablets of the Law were the most important. Our societies were built upon these stones. I understood the Negus for asking me what I was going to do with them, in the pit of my stomach I was beginning to feel a stirring, a new excitement. This was no inconsequential undertaking, I was no run-of-the-mill adventurer. I looked at my companions with intensity.

"Do you have a plan to get them out of the sacred cave?"

"It's not exactly a cave," Tafari said. "Let's say it's a chapel whose nave is cut out of living rock."

"And how are we going to get inside?"

Véronik took her brother's right hand in hers and showed it to me, holding it with care. It was slender and muscular, its fingers exceptionally long.

"Tafari is an artist. The Emperor enrolled him at the Beaux-Arts in Paris, where he has been studying for three years. My brother has talent and genius."

"You can see that caricatures are a habit with my sister," Tafari said quietly, hoping no doubt to redeem the jab about the shiny cassock and plastered-down hair.

Véronik turned to him.

"You can say what you like, your work is far better than what other artists in the kingdom are doing!" And to me, she added, "He has successfully infused the traditional Byzantine style with the magical power of the African soul. That's beyond argument. Tafari is Ethiopia's greatest painter, in spite of his young age."

Tafari himself continued: "It's an exaggerated reputation, of course, but that's why the Emperor was able to ordain that I should paint the ceiling of the holy chapel. This commission will serve as our pretext. I've already reserved the necessary scaffolding, materials, and tools. You will take care of the crates, which, if I ordered them, would have people wondering why I needed them. It's a fairly simple plan; we'll make adjustments as we go along. In a few days we'll have raised our tent, set up shop, and I'll begin work. Ten workers will help me, but in the evening, at sundown, they'll go home; you'll come and join me with Véronik; at the agreed moment, we'll act. I won't say any more just now."

I admired his concision.

"Your plan is simple and I like it. There's another side to the operation, though; how are we going to handle the tablets, get them out of the country? Dougherty suggested several routes. Can we talk about those?"

"We'll take a look at them," Véronik said. "We'll do whatever ground reconnaissance trips are necessary. We mustn't leave anything to chance."

Her face was so perfectly oval that she looked like one of those madonnas of which Rome has countless examples. The charm of the Armenian mother combined with the fine features of the Emperor had produced two magnificent, unique human beings. How could I convey my impression?

"Your mother must have been very beautiful," I said.

"She still is," retorted Véronik with the shadow of a pout, as though the compliment was superfluous.

"Another Bloody Mary? A whisky?"

Tafari raised an arm and snapped his fingers. The waiter appeared like a genie out of a bottle and placed more drinks on the table in front of us. To the tourists, businessmen, and call girls who had crowded into the bar, we must have looked like three young people who were together after a long separation. Surely, we must have met in one of the capital cities where the two of them had stayed. I felt tense because of the importance of the mission, and at the same time euphoric because of the presence of these two. Beauty is neither a right nor a supremacy, but when it's imparted so painlessly and totally, you have to know how to enjoy it. I was in beautiful company, in spirit as well as in body. Vodka must have had something to do with it, too.

"I won't be teaching you anything when I tell you that we're setting foot in an esoteric world," Tafari said to me.

"Which is hard to understand for someone who's not a mystic," Véronik added. "I warn you that for me, these stones are just stones, no more than that. My brother gets caught up in mythology."

"The tablets have a life of their own," Tafari continued. "It's said they can even put themselves across your path or help you in a magical way; they can also, if you ever try to take them in your hands, self-destruct and be no more than stone dust."

"I don't think we'll be at odds over that, God and I. I'm more afraid of the colonels' secret police," I said.

Tafari fell silent, thinking. Véronik tapped on the table in time to the music coming from the ceiling, and her gold bracelets sparkled against the brown skin of her bare arm in the darkness of the bar. Were we being watched?

"What we are undertaking is too huge for the secret police to have thought of it," Tafari said at last. "Anyway, the puts-chists are known, identified, even His Majesty knows who they are — a few colonels of the guard, as you've heard, Marxist students back from Germany, engineers back from Moscow, friends who met at night school at University College. They don't hold anything in particular against the Emperor, but against corruption, and the medieval clergy, and prevar-ication. The pot can't help but boil over. Do you know, as well, that two-thirds of the land belongs to the clergy? That, while the lions in the cage in front of the Ghebbi share quar-ters of meat, a large proportion of the people have nothing but spices to ward off their hunger?"

I looked at Véronik and Tafari with even more attention than before. I said sharply: "You're among the conspirators?"

"The die is already cast," Véronik replied. "Out of loyalty to our father, we have agreed to help you in this mission. It's his dearest wish to put his sacred tablets out of harm's way. After that, we'll see."

"It could even happen," Tafari said, putting his hand to his forehead (which I had seen the King of kings do repeatedly in Montreal — genetics will never cease to amaze me), "it could even happen that the disappearance of the tablets will light the fuse. Colonel Mengistu will claim that the Emperor has betrayed the kingdom, he'll robe himself in a lion's mane and declare the republic of Abyssinia. But by then you'll already be far away."

Tafari was mistaken. Events in reality moved faster than he had foreseen, but not as far. You could follow the street-fighting on television, and watch the tanks invade the intersections where, not so long before, I had been driving with Véronik at the wheel of her blue Volkswagen bug. The *Herald Tribune* that I bought this noontime at The Bookstore in Place Clemenceau, five minutes away from the Hôtel du Palais, gives one to believe that the old Emperor will survive this new putsch. Certain reports speak of a council of war that had decided to eliminate Hailé Selassie, but the people's affection for him still seems to protect him. The colonels will have to swallow their impatience, although the rest of the royal family, already decimated, is in exile on the Côte d'Azur. I hope Dougherty will go and pay them a visit, it would be rather nice.

For me here in Biarritz, writing my account of my mission, the days are going by faster than I would like. I still haven't tackled the most important episodes, and out of the two weeks I'd given myself to obtain a response from the Bank of the Holy Spirit five days have already passed. If the response to my demand is positive, this manuscript will never leave Eugénie's hotel, I shall burn it page by page in the fireplace in my room. However, if the Superior General of the Jesuits sends me a negative response, Moses himself will be turning in his grave.

4

TAFARI HAD SAID THAT A few days would be enough for him to have everything in place, four at most. I had ordered the wooden crates from a carpenter who worked for Mosvold and Co., a Swedish exporter. I had been promised them for the following Saturday but I couldn't count on that; everything was confirmed with the same phrase, "*ishy negeu*," meaning, "Of course, tomorrow." Ethiopians have an elastic sense of time, I couldn't play that game, I paid top price.

The morning after our nocturnal meeting, I was waiting for Véronik on the terrace of the King George, sipping an Ethiopian coffee, a *bounna*, for which I was acquiring a taste. The sun was hot and blinding. The sky was unbroken blue, the Negus had chosen the right time of year. I would not have wanted to haul the tablets through the mud of the rainy season, emptying the chapel as if it were an aquarium.

The Company of Jesus, I thought that morning, will most certainly claim the stones from me, for both scientific and historical reasons. How could I know what the Emperor had told Cardinal Sambrini? Had he simply asked for the Church's help, or had he been explicit? I believed he had not told the truth, otherwise Rome would not have let me leave alone, without chaperones.

Véronik arrived, driving her little blue Volkswagen with white-wall tires, which she parked diagonally on the shady side and entrusted to the care of a reformed thief who had left his two hands in prison for the same number of thefts. The laws being harsh, one was well advised not to get caught with one's fingers in the bag; her recidivist had been either stubborn or exceedingly hungry. He leaned against the car with his stumps crossed over his chest. Véronik had chosen her *zibagna* well; tall and stocky, he was still capable of kicking the beggars to drive them away. What would be cut off me if I was caught stealing the tablets? My tongue perhaps, because I'd conspired with the Emperor? The fingers that might have dared touch the words of God? My penis, because I'd felt the swell of desire to seduce Véronik? My eyes could also be burned out for having dared fall directly on the Torah. My head, for having conceived a diabolical plan? *Oh-h-h Alouette, gentille alouette.*

Véronik was coming toward me, the very image of an Abyssinian cat, lithe and untamed. She wasn't walking, she was undulating. I rose, flustered, seeming for certain like a ludicrous faithful admirer, drew back a chair for her, inviting her to be seated, taking her hand to shake it and not letting go, forgetting even to speak to her. She looked at me with a twinkle in her eye.

"You look funny, Father, are you feeling unwell?"

I let go of her hand and frowned. I had forbidden her to call me that.

"You know who you remind me of?" she continued. "An English lover I dumped, he was secretary at the United Kingdom embassy, charming, polite, but he thought I was so beautiful he spent hours just looking at me with his mouth open, as if I were an *objet d'art*. Love and admiration mustn't be confused."

Then she burst out laughing as she signalled a waiter to bring her a coffee. Nothing kills an erection like hearing about an ex-lover. I decided to attack.

"You're not my daughter, so why do you call me Father? And besides, it's true, you're really beautiful."

"Thank you, Monsieur Larochelle," she said. "But it would be more honest to admit there's a Casanova hiding under your cassock. You've left your Nordic realms in quest of the tablets, and now you consider it a fringe benefit to have me give you a chance of another conquest. That's the story."

"Don't judge a man by his clothes."

"Meaning?"

"I'm no more a believer than you are. I do belong to the Company, but it's a convenience."

"It's a lie, too."

Very beautiful women who know they're admired soon weary of seduction games. Véronik was a victim of her beauty; she never let down her guard. I tried to lighten the tone: "Perhaps you'd like me, as recommended by our founder, Saint Ignatius, to flagellate myself all night while thinking of you."

"One of your ancestors," she retorted, "Father Bourdaloue, I believe, seduced Madame de Sévigné with his Sunday sermons. I'm all ears, Father …"

"You're relentless!"

We weren't going to get very far this way. Fortunately, Véronik found the perfect ending: "My Englishman had more sense of humour than you …!"

That did it, I laughed at myself, at us. I do enjoy beginning a new relationship with a controlled aggression and neither Véronik nor I were willing to give up any ground. While we were attracted to one another, the male was not allowed to impose his dominance.

She drank down her coffee, in which she had allowed a cube of sugar to dissolve, a frown suddenly crossing her forehead.

"Let's go," she said briskly. "We've got work to do."

People who love action movies would never have the patience to build, step-by-step, the stages of the scenes that thrill them. Every adventurous undertaking demands fastidious preparation. We had to find a pickup truck in good condition with a canvas tarpaulin big enough to cover the two wooden crates; we needed several cans of gasoline, three would do; also rope, a box of tools, weapons and ammunition, spare tires with wheels already mounted. We spent two days at this, criss-crossing Addis in every direction. Véronik was well-acquainted with the merchants, but as we had to avoid rousing their curiosity, she introduced me as the manager of a travel agency that was organizing a hunting and photo safari, she said, for American press journalists. The pretext rang true, the fledgling tourist industry had no structures ready or able to provide service. I gave my contact information, the Imperial Ghion was a respected address. We succeeded in rounding up our essential supplies and even an Italian revolver, a Beretta .765, a jewel. What remained was to plot the get-away route.

By the third day, I knew all the paved roads and dirt lanes, the dry river beds that served for travel at this time of the year, and the tree-lined avenues leading to government buildings. The Bug flew along the main roads around the outskirts of the city while Véronik described the advantages and disadvantages of going by the Entoto Hills or taking the Asmara route. We quickly struck off the roads toward the great lakes, Dougherty had advised against them, too. There was not only road condition to consider, but a road's meandering pattern, the possibility of ambushes, and, above all, the estimated length of the journey. On certain routes, the distance–time relationship became astronomical.

I made use of our peregrinations to get to know Véronik better, I listened while she told me about her childhood at the palace, her favourite animals, and the day that came when the Emperor asked her mother, without rejecting her, to leave the court, politics taking precedence over love. My hand brushed against her thigh, she used the gear shift to deter my advances, very nearly breaking my fingers with the sudden change of gears. I learned gradually that she would more readily accept my gently caressing the back of her neck. Then she would relax and seemed to drive with more pleasure. Over lunch at a country inn, I finally had her facing me and her eyes were no longer avoiding mine.

"Last night," I said, "I read in *The Observer* the article on Ethiopian women you told me about. Do you really believe there's so little difference between Muslim and Coptic women?"

"Their situations are different, their alienation is the same. I'm one of those who's been lucky enough to get an education abroad, I understand better what an immense role the man plays in our country."

"Journalist and feminist too?"

"It's an art as well as an occupation. Being a woman is more important than having a press card."

"You write a lot?"

"Far too much, according to my father. I contribute to

foreign magazines, mostly, and I'm writing a book on the condition of women in third-world countries, real poverty, the most abject."

"You're astonishing."

"And you are especially flattering, you Jesuit inquisitor. I've told you about my loves, my studies, my journeys, even my ambitions, and you haven't yet told me anything about yourself. What do you do with your time when you're not in the service of the Emperor?"

"I try not to think too much. I accept the jobs the Provincial assigns me. I've taught but that doesn't seem to be my vocation, I have a lot of trouble following the plan of a textbook. So I roam about the world. I broaden my mind. I read. I run so as not to come face to face with God. That's it."

"You do believe in Him, then?"

"Less than Pascal."

"You're not very serious," Véronik said, her hands in her hair as if to put her thoughts back in place, "but I like your candour."

"Will you let me read your book?"

"That can't interest you," she replied, crossing her arms.

"Why, because I'm a man?"

"We're too different, you and I. A black cassock over a white skin has never made a half-breed. You're still a white. There's a boundary between us. I have no illusions ..."

A momentary sadness showed in her eyes. How could I get through to her? How could I bridge that barrier? I stroked her cheek with my fingertips, she took my hand and very gently kissed it in the hollow of the palm. Then we ate the dish that was served us, in silence as if at a convent table.

By the end of the third day, we no longer had any secrets from one another but we still had not found the sought-for route. Before going back to the city, I asked her to stop the car, I wanted to climb a rock that overlooked the valley, but a few steps up the slope I carelessly put my foot in a nest of red ants, which invaded me all the way up into my underpants. Véronik saw me dance naked in the sun and the dust. I didn't appreciate her uncontrollable laughter, but the creatures had, shall I say, gobbled up the reticence we'd had with each other.

That evening, we dined at the hotel, drank a little champagne, and nibbled at some venison brochette with sauced noodles. Then Véronik came up to the room with me, where we spread our road maps on the bed and concluded that none of the potential routes were satisfactory.

"What it comes down to," she said, removing the cute little magnifying glasses through which she had been examining the maps, "is that there's only one possible way of getting out of Addis Ababa undetected … by our one and only railway line, Addis-Djibouti."

She looked at me resolutely, a little thoughtfully. I like brainy women. She was becoming more and more seductive.

I ordered wine brought up, I was feeling like James Bond for sure. Véronik kept working.

"You'll drive the pickup to the station, you'll spend the night there, and in the wee hours of the morning you'll have the crates loaded on a railway car. It'll cost a little money, some *gourshas* to oil the cogs, but I think it'll work. And then I'll join you to head off communication problems."

"You're really rejecting the route through Eritrea?"

"The trip would be too long, with far too many uncertainties."

We agreed to consult Tafari for the final decision.

"What time is it?" Véronik asked.

It was ten o'clock.

"We'll see my brother tomorrow at noon, then."

The wine arrived. The bottle was lying in a bucket that was too big and the cork was floating in the icy water. I watched Véronik serve us, she was talking with her hands. The desire in me was following its course.

We clinked glasses, she burst out laughing.

"What is it that's so funny?"

"I was thinking of poor *Homo sapiens sapiens*, whom you could meet up with in the Awash Basin."

"I promise I'll say hello."

"I was telling myself," Véronik continued, "that he'd surely be worried to see you carting around God's Commandments when he himself has lived for millions of years without the Creator having a thing to say to him."

"Do you think the Garden of Eden was in the valley of the Awash? That would be pretty fantastic."

"Possible," she said, "that Adam could have been a chimpanzee."

"Or a gorilla? Or orangutan?"

"Certainly a primate," she said, "we're all descended from the same fossil."

She stopped talking. We were face to face, I felt a flush of heat envelop us despite the cool night air.

"Véronik," I said, "do you think you have to go home tonight?"

She smiled and folded up the maps lying open on the bed, untied her shoes, and poured us more cooled wine without even trying to stifle the yawns that added a new dash of intimacy to the pouring. I stroked the back of her neck, gently, the way I had in the car. She stood up, stretching, and went to the window, her back to me. I came close and for a moment held her by the hips, like an amphora, then kissed her neck and slowly undressed her, one item at a time: blouse, skirt, shoes, panties, bra, without her turning around, the way one undresses a mannequin in a shop window. Her shoulders received my first caresses. Her curves were exquisite. She opened the balcony door, the air was cool, the city lit up, naked in the night, supported by both hands, she leaned with back arched against the railing.

Never had there been as many hormones in my blood, never had I undressed as fast, never had the adipose tissues of my penis swelled so full. We stayed glued to one another for long minutes, we talked, we kissed, on the balcony of the Imperial Ghion we took the same position over and over with the same wave-like movements, our eyes among the stars, no longer on the planet Earth.

When the air began to cool, the night wind rising perhaps, we went inside, we stood before the big wardrobe mirror, happy to see ourselves together from head to toe. We found we were a beautiful sight, astonished at the colours of our skins and the light in our eyes.

"It would be a shame to let the night die," whispered Véronik.

I made do with the usual inanities men pronounce while I led her to the bed, where we behaved as prescribed by the law of thirtysomethings with eternity ahead of them.

5

THE NEXT MORNING WE REACHED Tafari by telephone. He was not going to be free until sundown, so we agreed to eat together at a popular restaurant in the mercato run by an Italian friend of his. It should be known that after the Second World War a number of Mussolini's infantrymen had decided to stay in the country rather than return to a devastated Italy. Perhaps they were not all yearning to go back to the missus and kids and the old routine. They took native wives, set up in business, import-export, trucking, mechanics, restaurants. They integrated into the life of the old city, some even opened butcher shops and groceries. How was this small merchant bourgeoisie going to resist the blowing Marxist winds? Did the rest of the white community — Armenian, Greek, or Lebanese — support the Emperor or the revolutionaries?

"They're under pressure from both sides," Véronik told

me, "and increasingly. My stepfather is very worried, but Maman doesn't want to leave the country."

"And you?"

She shrugged her shoulders, adding: "I'm also the king's daughter."

We went to take possession of a pickup truck, half Chevrolet, half Mercedes, fixed up by a brilliant mechanic, which I drove as well as I could through the hilly streets of the capital, the Bug following behind. Once I thought I was mastering the vehicle, I returned to the hotel, where I stopped it in a shady corner of the parking lot. The *zibagna*, a veteran of the battles that had liberated the country, was still wearing his old British uniform, which was torn, patched, and resewn, but he carried himself with pride, and the *baksheesh* I placed in his palm won me a faithful ally.

Véronik had gone up to the room ahead of me, but it wasn't magical like the previous night, or even passionate. I think we were beginning to feel the approach of the big test. Our senses were not playing along, time was slipping between our fingers, and even desire was in short supply. I was dumb enough to ask her if she would rather have been in bed with her embassy secretary. Primal jealousy, neanderthal level.

In a diatribe I deserved, she flung at me, "You're all the same!" In her eyes, I represented the male rabble worldwide. "You want to seduce us, possess us, penetrate us, make us come, come yourselves, and on top of that you want points, to be ranked, like in school, you want to be top of the class, the best lover, unforgettable! There are times — and this is one of them — when I find you really hard to take. Why not just be satisfied with the relationship you yourself created? We had a pretty good interaction, didn't we? Was last night one out of the storybooks?"

"Never since my vows of chastity have I lived hours so intense."

She didn't laugh. She was right. Why would I roam the world wondering if the heart and body hidden under my cassock were better than those possessed by the Franciscans, Dominicans, Eudists, or Benedictines of the earth?

Véronik still hadn't let go when we had a drink together in Beltrami's back courtyard under a sterile banana tree, with the city's clamour all around us.

"Love, Michel, is a relationship, it's not a conquest, so you can come down off your high horse. You're not a dandelion spreading its seed to the four winds. I know your male mission is to perpetuate the race, but it seems to me we're past the time when people saw no connection between sexuality and fertility. It gives me as much pleasure to drink this Cinzano with you as to feel you on my belly ..."

"What did you think when we saw each other for the first time in the Ghion bar?"

I was fishing for compliments.

"I didn't think: I'm going to put a Jesuit in my specimen book. That's not the way women figure. What I thought when I saw you was that the Emperor had described you well — open face, young, good looking. I thought that we would be friends. That I was going to like working with you. That's all."

"But we went further."

What was I hoping for? We were at a crossroads.

"You insisted. If you hadn't, I would never have gone up to your room. I had no need to make love. It was once we were joined that my body felt like rejoicing. Do you understand?"

I was having trouble understanding. If everything in life were only interaction, I still had a lot to learn about women.

"May I be indiscreet?" Véronik asked. "Why did you join the Company of Jesus? Sincerely?"

On the courtyard's vine-covered picket fence, a rooster was getting ready to crow.

"What did it was Boy Scout novels, Don Quixote, gallant knights, Gulliver exploring the world, Lewis Carroll opening the doors of Wonderland for me, and all those musketeer adventures. I told you, didn't I, that my mother left Papa to look after me and he nurtured me on literature? It was the adventurers who ploughed the seas for a good cause that most caught my imagination. They had an ideal. They transmitted it to me through their battles on the printed page. At eighteen, I was still a virgin and I dreamed of changing the world! You won't find a single classified ad looking for a righter of wrongs, with opportunities for travel, exploration of continents, intervention in crises. Papa's advice, he was right, was that the Jesuits, with their rules, their reputation, their energy, would open the ranks of a crusading army for me ..."

"But then the novitiate, the priesthood, the vows of poverty, of chastity, that was literature?"

"Drama. We're on a stage, I assume my roles."

"And after thieving, lying, hating, extorting, after fucking, making love, how can you wear the habit?"

"I confess myself. I give myself absolution. Since it's always in exceptional situations, I won't wait till I've found a confessional and confessor; I forgive myself."

Véronik looked at me as if thunderstruck, she must have been wondering if I was fabricating a Jesuit to fit the bill, just for her. The rooster began to crow, but without literature I would never have crossed the threshold of the seminary! I was adamant.

"You mean to say," she declared finally, looking me straight in the eye, "that you traded me for two expiatory rosaries?!"

Mercifully, Tafari arrived at this point, slipping onto a chair beside me; he shook my hand, winked at his sister. He looked exhausted, his shoulders slightly rounded, traces of earth on his face.

"Everything's in place," he told us, "it hasn't been easy. I haven't worked this hard for a long time. All that's left is to have the palace approve the sketch of what I'm supposed to put on the chapel ceiling. I'm rather proud of it. Would you like to see?"

Then he took three small sheets of tracing paper out of a folder and laid them one over another on the restaurant table. It was magnificent, in India ink and watercolour, a brilliant transposition of the Ark of the Covenant, a design harking back to the earliest conception of a single God and yet rejoicing in contemporary spirituality. There were touches of purple, violet, red, and crimson, the colours of the ancestral faith; at the four corners of the ceiling, golden cherubs clustered about the crossbeams; the whole scene was bathed in a heavenly cloud. This fresco was going to transfigure the room.

"It's superb," I said to Tafari, "and the synod is sure to tell you to go ahead."

"I told you my brother was a genius!" added Véronik, clapping her hands.

She was addressing me with the formal *vous* that we had used when we met, out of modesty perhaps. Or was our relationship being skewed by Tafari's presence?

"How are you going to turn down the chance to do this painting?" I asked her brother.

"I'll do it someday. Meanwhile, we've got other fish to fry. I'm hungry."

Tafari signalled to his friend, Antonio Cerio, if I remember correctly, who made us an artichoke salad, Bismarck beefsteak, and roast potatoes, and served us a red wine from his native Tuscany.

"Véronik," I said, lowering my voice, "thinks the safest route is the railway."

"It's the oldest," Tafari replied.

"I suggest," Véronik added, "that we send the crates from Addis to the station at Dire Dawa. After a short stop, Monsieur Larochelle will take the train again for Djibouti. Seven hundred and twenty-eight kilométres."

"It's certainly closer than the port of Assab. And it's true, the roads are less and less reliable," Tafari said. "Yesterday, between Addis and Djimma, four tourists were killed and their car was burned."

"You agree about using the train and the port of Djibouti?"

"That means two things …"

But we were interrupted by the arrival of dinner. Tafari ate heartily, I drank wine as if I had twenty masses to celebrate, Véronik hardly ate anything; if her brother had not been there, I would have asked her if our coming separation was weighing on her. I would have liked her to explain to me why, when a relationship ends, it's the man who suffers most. Because his pride is wounded? Or in punishment for having seduced without forethought? We were at a small table, I felt her leg against mine. Tafari was focused on our plan: "First, we'll only send one crate to Dire Dawa, the other must stay here. It would be madness to ship the Abouna and his bodyguard. If they come to, they'll alert the whole countryside. They could die of thirst in that crate. We have to find a safe place to shut them up in.

"Second, merchandise is shipped on Mondays and Wednesdays. There's only one track. The same train does the outbound and return trip. That means that we'll attack on Sunday night, you'll be with the tablets over forty-eight hours. It's risky, but from Dire Dawa you can go up to Harar, Rimbaud's stamping ground, it's very close. You'll pick up the crate again and get back on the train with it on Wednesday. Does that suit you?"

"This jaunt with the sacred stones is going to be a long one," I said. "If Yahweh wants to complicate life for me, he doesn't have to look far …"

"There's no other solution, I'm sure of it. Trust my intuition!"

Véronik was smiling, our relationship was back on track. For how long?

"Where are we going to take the people crate?" Tafari asked.

"We mustn't get the two mixed up," I said. "Put a cross on the one with the tablets. We're in a Christian country …"

"Which reminds me," Veronik's brother piped up. "Behind the students' dormitory, the college has a storeroom."

"I'll look after it," I said. "I promised myself I'd go and visit my colleagues before leaving. I'll go tomorrow. Véronik will tell them I'm here, as if I've just arrived. I don't want my brothers to know I've been at the Imperial Ghion all this time."

"Tell them you're living with us, that our stepfather is a friend of your father's, make it up."

"I don't even know where you live."

"Behind the cathedral, a big wooden house, the Villa Boghossian. Okay?"

I had no difficulty meeting the principal of the college, a Jesuit from Canada who had been in this country for twenty years. Was he wearing a hair shirt or was he working in cahoots with the military experts the United States had delegated to His Majesty? He had known the Emperor for so long that he claimed to be able to consult him whenever he wished.

Father Méridien was delighted to show me around the college, have me meet the students in their French classes, visit the laboratories and the library. I was deferent to the tips of my fingernails. I asked the right questions at the right moments. The old Jesuit told me that the Muslim students were the best, but the directive was to encourage the little Catholics, even by cheating. At coffee time, I met the teachers gathered in a common room, as they did twice a day to exchange information and nibble on biscuits. Together, they were a unit of battle-hardened soldiers convinced that their presence on these high plateaus was enabling them to play a role in history.

After introducing me to his colleagues, Father Méridien claimed the floor.

"*Ad majorem Dei gloriam!*" he said, his eyes cast downward, his hands folded one over the other, standing in the middle of the room, the walls hung with class photographs, all taken on the steps leading to the front door, all alike, a row of teachers sitting on straight chairs, Méridien in an armchair at the centre, the graduating class on the steps in order of size. Here and there, a few faces of young girls lit up the group, but the black-and-white pictures were all overexposed, as if the official college photographer only had a pre-war-vintage Kodak box camera.

The choir of Jesuits repeated the invocation of the greatest glory of God, and Méridien continued: "Gentlemen, friends, Father Larochelle has come to visit us without having advised us of his arrival a week ago in Addis Ababa, where he has been staying with our friends the Boghossians. The father is here on a mission, for which His Majesty has personally brought him to the country."

Then he turned to me and recited an oration that must have been the classic tailored to the occasion: "Father, we are here for God, for education, and because the Emperor asked us to serve him. You know that since Menelik, the uncle of the Ras Makonnen, the French language is the first language of the Empire. It is less true today, English has taken precedence, but in loyalty, His Majesty went and sought French Canadians to found this college and his university. We are happy to see that the tradition is still alive and that the King of kings went to Montreal to choose a Jesuit, from whom he expects the greatest loyalty. We shall pray for you, you will do the same for us because the times are difficult, yesterday, again one of our fathers was attacked in the mercato, which not long ago was something never seen. Rebellion is brewing, we will do all in our power to aid the Emperor and Christ. Amen."

The choir chimed in, "Amen," and then Méridien added as postscript that if any fathers wished to benefit from my brief presence to be confessed, I would of course be available.

Thus it was that for three-quarters of an hour I found myself behind a makeshift grill, listening to the turpitudes of the community. One was masturbating daily, another had molested a student in exchange for good marks, yet another had knocked over a child in the street with his Fiat but had not stopped to take him to the hospital — a pitiful case, whose breath, reeking of alcoholic fumes, left little doubt over the state in which he must drive his car, teach his classes, deal with his guilt — two good fathers were regularly stealing money from the procuracy and library to spend at the brothel. I pardoned, imposed penitences, invoked divine grace.

At the end of the afternoon, I asked Méridien to introduce me to the coadjutor brother in charge of administration of the college. We visited the grounds, and I obtained a key to the main gate and one for the storeroom. I had, I explained to them, a few documents to put in a safe place in the days to come. Father Méridien told me that the following Sunday all the Jesuits were leaving for Harar, as they did every year, to spend the Easter holidays in a villa they rented on the outskirts of the city.

"I shall stop by to say hello without fail," I announced to him before leaving. "I've decided not to take the plane, but the train, to see something of the country."

When I rejoined Véronik on the terrace of the King George, where she was reading under a parasol as she waited for me, I reported to her that our project was looking most propitious.

"What are you reading?"

"Rimbaud, *Illuminations*," she told me, "which I haven't picked up since I was in convent in Switzerland. All he wrote is extraordinary, of course, but it's even more extraordinary to reread it at my age, between love and death."

"What do you mean?"

"It could very well be that you were my last relationship. Rumour has it that the northwestern tribes will rebel before the end of the month. I'm going to enlist, put myself at the service of the officers of the Guard, I shall be killed at some street corner, perhaps over there, at the foot of the liberation monument."

"I can hardly imagine you as a soldier," I said. "Not that you couldn't fight, but it seems to me His Majesty has prepared you for other things — organization, writing, persuasion — things that have nothing to do with explosions, grenades, whistling bullets, thudding bazookas. Don't you believe that?"

I began to gaze dreamily and sadly at the stone lion that rose above the square. How many Ethiopians had died in the battles they waged against Marshal Graziani's troops? The remains of some of the victims had been placed in a common grave under the cathedral. The Emperor had given instructions that he himself should be buried inside those walls, beside the Menen.

I drew close to Véronik, her face was sad. A gentle tenderness suffused us.

"I love you," she said. "Forgive me."

Would she be in Biarritz with me today if she had turned down the call to arms? There was a smouldering passion in her like a bed of coals that was fanned by the gross injustice of her birth. As the natural child of the Negus Negushi, the King of kings, she wanted to take to her heart the children of the street, who never ate their fill, who would not learn to read, who had no hope. She sensed her lot as if it were guilt, and bore the weight of her duty as she saw it on her shoulders.

I never thought to ask her if she had come with the Emperor to Europe on his return from Canada. Had she taken a dip in the huge pool at the Hôtel du Palais? I can readily imagine her swimming toward me, leaping out of the water, shaking herself, then coming to dry her magnificent hair beside me. We would have explored the fish restaurants, bet on Jai-Alai games as tourists dazzled by the prowess of the players, we would have travelled into the mountains, all the way to the snows of the Pyrenees. I was thinking in a callow, conventional way, undoubtedly, like an idealistic teenager. For Véronik, there could be no refusal to go to the barricades. And for us, there was now no turning back: the theft of the tablets was set for the following Sunday evening.

6

WHEN WE ARRIVED AT THE monastery in the pickup truck, Tafari was perched on a ladder leading to the scaffolding under the ceiling. He carried on as if he heard nothing. Four hours earlier, the workmen had put down their tools and, on their way home, gone off to the bars to visit the girls. The favourite drink there was *tedj*, a honey-based alcohol fermented with *gesho* that gave monumental headaches to whites.

We had agreed to mimic surprise, like disoriented tourists arriving inadvertently at a sanctuary, and to take the bishop and his armed bodyguard unawares at the entrance to the tabernacle, beneath the chapel ceiling. We had to seize them one after the other, first the soldier, who came toward me. Véronik had hidden behind the truck. I pretended to be looking for a road, the fellow pointed his automatic rifle at me, I offered him a cigarette, then a match, and babbled something while showing him my road map.

When he had decided there was no danger, the guard put down his gun, grabbed the map, and opened it wide, upside down. It was clear he could not read but wanted to impress me. At this very moment, Tafari threw himself from the top of the ladder onto the fellow's back. Stunned, the bodyguard rolled on the ground, and Véronik was quick to give him a sure knockout blow with a club. She had brought ropes, which we used to tie him up, trussed like a ham. She gagged him with surgical tape, and we hauled him off toward a corner of the chapel until it was time to hoist him into the crate.

The Abouna panicked — he could see little through the smoke of incense, night was falling, everything made darker still by the great eucalyptus trees bordering the grounds — he had lost his bodyguard and turned in circles, protesting angrily. All three of us were short of breath from our efforts but also breathing hard like fighters, I was afraid, I felt my rib cage tightening. The patriarch suddenly tore off his headdress, a kind of black silk turban, and began to yell like a trapped animal. Tafari leapt forward to shut him up. The old man, now like a hyena, yelled harder, backing away toward the Ark of the Covenant, head lowered, vicious-looking. At first, Tafari grabbed him by the shoulders. He struggled, Tafari then took the priest by the neck. The priest suffocated, all he was breathing anymore was incense. I don't think Tafari really squeezed his fingers but he well and truly strangled the old man, who passed from life to death in a few seconds, by the light of the chapel's candles that gleamed on the brocade of his robes.

Véronik and I went to join Tafari, the patriarch was lying on the ground like a rag. Tafari turned to us: "This isn't exactly what we'd planned," he muttered with distaste.

"We'll talk about that later. Help me carry him to the crate," I called.

We were in a terrible jam.

Véronik turned to the bodyguard while Tafari and I were heaving the old man. When we came back to join her, we heard her say: "We can't leave this one alive, he could recognize us, denounce us."

"The bishop's death was an accident," I said. "Leave this one to me, I'll confess myself."

I could have cut his throat, like a sheep's, with the knife I always carried now but I didn't want any blood; a silk thread stopped his breathing for good. The three of us had all we could handle getting him into the wooden crate, henceforth a coffin for the two of them. In a week, the good fathers, on returning from their Easter holidays, would find the bodies in their storeroom. So much for the reputation of the Company of Jesus! Father Méridien, who pretended to be one of the Emperor's circle of friends, would be hard-pressed to extricate himself from this situation. I can see him now, that fat little man with the flattened nose, insisting he knew nothing of the murder. He would be white with rage and denounce the Islamic extremists, knowing full well that sometimes Jesuits too had blood on their hands.

The most important part remained to be done. Tafari and I went back into the chapel, leaving Véronik to stand guard, armed with the soldier's automatic rifle. She stationed the truck pointing toward the way out, doors open, motor running, in case of need for quick departure. Sitting on the front bumper, between the lit headlights, she was invisible but could see everything in their beams, which covered the entire road and surrounding bushes all the way to the stone gate.

Tafari and I found a room lit by beeswax candles, searched the drawers there, lifted tanned, oiled-leather coverings, and unfolded scented wrappings of gold-threaded cloth beneath, finally to place our hands on two enormous stones covered back and front with small writings.

"That's not Ge'ez," Tafari said, "it's Hebrew."

"I think Moses was very strong and very lazy. When God dictated his law to him as a punishment, Moses thought: I'll transcribe it all in a minimum of space and transport the Ten Commandments in jig time. We'll do likewise."

Tafari helped me lift one of the tablets, and I carried it to the truck, breathing hard and practically staggering under the load. I hurried back to help Tafari carry the second tablet; he couldn't do it alone, an artist, not as sturdy as I. With the leather and cloth we nested and steadied them, five thousand years of annotated texts, an original certainly, something of great value to the librarians of Jerusalem. We closed up the two crates with mighty hammer blows, nailing on the covers, which dropped perfectly into their settings.

Despite the feverishness that had gripped the three accomplices, at the moment he left us, Tafari found it in him to add: "You know that one of the Commandments, I don't know which, tells mankind: 'Thou shalt not kill'?"

He pulled a face in chagrin.

Véronik shrugged: "I don't see why God would say 'thou' to me. That's like *tu*. We haven't been introduced. Come, gentlemen, we haven't finished our work. As long as the tablets aren't on board the train, I won't sleep."

It was almost eleven o'clock, it would soon be midnight, the curfew had sounded long ago.

"They died quickly and gave their lives to protect a legend. In the crate, they would have given up their souls with greater suffering. Tafari, revolutions don't happen without ..."

Night had fallen and the silence of the forest enveloped us. Tafari remained still. He smiled at me, we embraced. There was no need now for him to risk his talent further.

I promised myself as we parted that one day I would buy paintings of his, I would collect them for their beauty, but also out of friendship. I imagined myself too as a magi arriving from Abyssinia, bearing incense, and gold, and works of art.

When Tafari had left, Véronik took the wheel and drove us through back streets to the college, where I opened the gate, then we went to the storeroom and backed the truck inside. We hadn't allowed for the weight of the prisoners; the crate fell on the floor and broke, like the tablets that Moses had thrown on the ground in his anger with the idolaters. The bodies tumbled out of the box, the patriarch pathetic in his silken robes, the soldier like a punished child. We closed the doors, I didn't have the courage to put them back in their rough wooden coffin. In a few nights, the jackals, drawn by the smell of rot, would alert the curious.

As we left, Véronik came close to me on the seat and put her hand on my arm. I thought at once of my first advances. Our encounter had happened on a razor's edge. Ten days of work, worries, discovery — an adventure that had sharpened our senses and minds.

"A shame we have to part," she said, squeezing my wrist as if encouraging my attachment. "We could have lived together."

"You mean," I replied, "behaved like civilized people, talking about the news, going to the movies to see the latest Godard?"

"Making babies, laughing and crying. But it won't be that way. The Muslims have a word for it …"

I rejected the idea of a tragic destiny. Not Véronik. Was this our different languages or cultures? The philosophy of the snows opposed to the philosophy of the sands? I knew it was pointless to argue.

So as not to arrive too early at the station, I proposed a detour by the hotel, where I had kept my room. The parking-lot guardian was happy to see us, I represented his sole daily tip, he lay down at the foot of the Mercedes while we went up to relax for a few hours. Of course, a shower. Of course a kiss. We gazed at each other till we could no longer see, but we did not make love. The relationship was over. I fell asleep beside a revolutionary who no longer had time for indulgence in bodily fantasies.

The alarm clock buzzed at four o'clock, we dressed quickly and ran to the truck. The guardian received his *baksheesh* and huddled himself up in his shamma, which was still pulled over his uniform because the night was cold. The sun was already showing through the stratus clouds when we passed through the iron gate of the Ghion and sped toward the station. Even at this early morning hour, with no makeup or preening, in the rough, as it were, Véronik was more beautiful than the day that was rising over the mimosas and dragon trees.

The rear courtyard of the Franco-Ethiopian railway's Main Railway Station was jammed with miscellaneous packages, carts, sacks of coffee, among which dozens of haggard coolies were threading, along with early risen passengers concerned most of all with not losing sight of their suitcases and roped-up boxes. The enormous clock on the wall, in the purest Art Deco style, was showing 2:12.

"It stopped the day of my birth," said Véronik, laughing,

"and hasn't dared start again since. Which explains why I never age."

The Addis Ababa station, inaugurated on June 7, 1917, was a monument of steel and wood that in any other country would have been classified a national treasure. Plain to see, it had been built with the scrap from the Eiffel Tower.

Tafari had told me about it.

"For the first time, you'll be seeing a three-dimensional design by the architect Carzou, a sharp-edged model."

He was to take the early-morning Blue Nile Line plane for Khartoum, first of all. He was so often in the airport that his being there would arouse no suspicion. It was agreed among us not to try to make contact again.

"What's the Emperor going to say about the operation?" I asked Véronik. "How's he going to take the news of the two bodies?"

"Not to worry," she whispered, "I'll take care of that, I'll go and see him tomorrow, at an hour that will give you a bit of a head start. I don't think he'll send his troops after you. He's got other and better things to do. And let's be honest, two deaths aren't a matter of state in the kingdom. As far as the tablets are concerned, I think he'll manage to cool the scandal. After all, he's the one who wanted them out of the country."

A locomotive began to give off steam, cars knocked together, steel against steel. We backed the truck up to a ramp,

Véronik left to find coolies to transfer the crate to a platform that was beginning to overflow with merchandise. I waited in this bedlam, my pulse beating hard, leaning against a steel column, its bolts digging into my shoulder. An electric crane passed back and forth over my head without ever stopping.

Véronik had soon taken care of the inevitable paperwork to be filled in, and distributed the necessary money, a smile here and a few thalers there, four sturdy porters deposited the crate at the end of the car that was to detach from the train at Dire Dawa. The idea had occurred to us simply to write *Tables* on the shipping form, the French word for tables and stone tablets as well. I could always say I was taking furniture made in the country to an exhibition of crafts. It would tickle God's funny bone! A sleepy customs officer applied an export sticker on the side of the crate with starch paste that he spread generously with large swipes of a brush. All that remained was to make sure I had a seat in the last car. Véronik came with me to the wicket, time was passing and we only had a few minutes left to share. Out of her bag she took the edition of *Illuminations*, wrapped in its tissue paper.

"Read Rimbaud and think of me," she said.

My leaving gave our separation a pall of finality. She did no more than touch my hand, she was biting her lips, her face inscrutable. I didn't dare say the trite things that came to my mind. The train was supposed to leave Addis Ababa at seven o'clock, but it was past eight when the departure whistle blew. I jumped aboard the car and sat by the window. The train started, it was so heavy that the wheels of the locomotive skidded, like the paws of a big dog pulling on his chain, then in a burst of steam, there was a jerk on the collar and we began to move, first at a walk, then at a trot. Véronik was still watching me, her hand raised. I could read on her lips an *au revoir*, till we meet again, that would never happen. I kept watching her till a bend in the track cut off our view of each other. I was the one the car was taking away, but it was she who was leaving me. I was, and remain, inconsolable.

Véronik was wedded to an era and a cause, she belonged to no man. Over a few days she had taught me to live. In her, there was such lucidity blended with such beauty that never will I find a cocktail to match it in any other woman. I had felt my cynicism melt in her presence like snow in the sunshine of April. This separation was the first crack in my career plan.

We were sitting, crammed together, on uncomfortable wooden benches, the aisle of the car was strewn with tin food containers, chickens tied by the feet, hobbled baby pigs, multicoloured packages. Frightened by the mechanical noises, the old men, the women, and the children kept silent, they who were used to riding donkey-back, as when Jesus was alive.

The warm morning air and the locomotive smoke that invaded us in puffs made one thirsty. I bought a bottle of

St. George from a boy, swallowed several gulps of the luke-warm beer, and let my mind wander, fascinated by the label showing the saint dispatching a loathsome dragon with his lance. St. George Beer. How could we accept having a sacred myth turned into an advertizing icon? Saint George, my cousin, my brother, how far would I go to find peace? To whom should I pray for the strength to go as far as I must with the Tablets of the Law? Hadn't I read somewhere that they had been destroyed at the same time as the temple of Jerusalem? Were there really two sets? Was I in the process of making a fool of myself?

The locomotive gradually reached a rapid pace and we travelled through lush greenery along the course of the Awash River, which ran parallel to the railway line. Huge crocodiles could be seen in the river, and hunters risking their lives for hides from which luxurious handbags would be made. Farther on, in the savannah, zebras and giraffes, buffalos and gazelles looked as if they'd emerged straight out of a book by Edgar Rice Burroughs. Or perhaps the Garden of Eden.

From my safari, I was bringing back trophies of another age. I was a great hunter in God's domain, and I was sleeping heavily, my head against the varnished-wood window frame of a swaying, lurching railway car made twenty years earlier by a company called Établissments Billards in the city of Tours, in France.

When I woke, everything had changed, a few thatch-roofed *tukouls* dotted the countryside, the river had disappeared, following its own course, here and there a herdsman could be seen, a long stick over his shoulder, tending a herd of zebus and young goats. The goats were climbing the trees to glean their last remaining green leaves. The rainy season would not be far off now, but drought had already yellowed and scorched the earth, famine was threatening. The Dankali depression spread its phosphorescent colours before our eyes, outcroppings of sulphur showed as patches of lemon yellow and burnt orange, the earth itself revealing wild-animal semblances. My weather-forecasting network would have served no purpose, Dougherty was right indeed.

At sunset, we came in sight of Dire Dawa, my journey was not over, but I had stopped feeling constantly threatened. I left my precious cargo under customs bond, protected by two railway guards.

7

THE GOOD FATHERS WERE STAYING in a villa near Harar, they had given me the address. I decided to go and take a rest there, and entrusted my young life to an old taxi. The house was at the top of a hill that the car was unable to climb, the road's stones had been worn so smooth. I covered the final one hundred metres on foot, and found a huge dwelling outrageously lit up, like a midnight sun in the neighbour-hood. It was a modern cement block building with a sloping roof and wide verandas all around. On the staff at the roof ridge, there was a flag the colour of which I could not distinguish in the darkness; a radio-telephone antenna was visible against the sky.

As I approached, I saw shadows through the windows moving against the walls of a room where my confreres were feasting. When I opened the double doors, I was greeted with hurrahs as hearty as if I had won an Olympic medal.

They were fifteen at table, two servers were carrying trays, the plates were empty, the knives, forks, and spoons had been laid to rest, the brothers were now into the cognac and visibly somewhat tipsy. At each end of the table sat a Jesuit of note: Father Méridien of course, as head of the troops and rector of the college, and facing him, to my great delight, Father Rodriguez, my teacher, who rose and came to greet me.

"So, Larochelle, you didn't expect to find me here, did you?"

I thought he was in California with his dancer, I told him, tongue in cheek, busy working up a musical comedy produced by Gene Kelly! I added that I'd thought he was done for but should have suspected the whole business was just an invention of the devil.

Privately, Rodriguez said to me: "You must admit, it was a wonderful excuse to give the slip to my colleagues in Cairo! They had no further need of me, but by then didn't want to let me leave. My ignominious departure will remove any desire to have me back with them. And you? What's been happening with you? Are you still following my advice?"

During my retreat at the Ricci house, Rodriguez had been my mentor, my director of conscience, my lifebuoy, and an indefatigable conversational partner. At the time, I was worried because I believed neither in God nor in Satan, and what attracted me most in the proposals of the Company was the hotel-type living.

Rodriguez was entirely of the same mind, he told me. I had chosen right in obeying my father. I was offered a career filled with unpredictable experiences, freedom, and security. Food, lodging, laundry, a hundred colleges around the world, a stimulating intellectual life, the exotic, the erotic, respect from aboriginal peoples, what more could a young fellow ask? Faith? Faith was a gift. Who knew what winding paths the Lord followed? There were those who embraced the priesthood because they had heard a divine call, and the others who followed a path with patience.

These were the words of a friend. I decided on the patient path, I chose the cassock, but I kept the trousers.

At the end of the spiritual exercises of Saint Ignatius, Rodriguez even initiated me to bourbon on the rocks as he explained to me that certain novices belonged to certain special forces.

"This Company was founded by a gentleman at the very time that Rabelais was publishing his greatest books. His disciples influenced kings and enthralled the masses. You will be in good company."

I was once again facing this man who had enabled me to fulfill myself and break out of the narrow world of my birth. When I think that I might have been a notary! Rodriguez had aged a smidgen and seemed to me a little stooped, with grey hairs bristling around his ears, and some new wrinkles no doubt inflicted by his belly dancer, for there are never rumours without some foundation of truth.

"I've just come from Addis Ababa, as you know," I said to him.

"You have baggage, can we get it for you at the station?" My teacher was pressing me.

"I'd like to borrow one or two good cassocks. I'm coming back to civilization. For the rest, I have everything in my backpack, I always travel the way you taught me to, ready for any departure."

Méridien interrupted loudly from the end of the table: "And your mission for the Emperor. You've accomplished it?"

Rodriguez smiled. The chattering and laughing ceased, and the diners fell silent, all leaning toward me as if I were about to reveal the presence of Christ to them. I didn't know what Rodriguez knew of the operation. What had Méridien told him about my being in Addis Ababa? And what was Rodriguez doing in Harar anyway? Was he here to help me or bring me into line? He was my teacher and friend, but the first lesson he had taught me was to be on my guard. I decided to proceed as if everyone knew that I was working for the Metra system, period.

"Yes indeed, everything went magnificently, I got the aid promised and we signed our contract."

"The Boghossians are still up there?" Méridien asked.

"Tafari took a Sudan Airways plane this morning for Frankfurt, via Khartoum. I think he's going to open an exhibition. Véronik stayed with her mother. She's afraid there's going to be a people's revolt and wants to be with her for the aftermath."

I was handling this pretty well. Of course, we were all of us specialists in mental restriction.

"You must be hungry. I'll get you a bite," Rodriguez pronounced, then turning to a server. "Set a place for Father Larochelle and bring him a brochette and some salad with a bottle of that bracing Chianti."

Then he had me sit beside him, adding: "You couldn't know what we were discussing at the very moment you arrived."

"The art of belly dancing?" I suggested facetiously, as is appropriate at these group meals where teasing is a forerunner to cruelty.

"No, although the subject is not without interest in an Arab country," Rodriguez replied, "we were talking about the man who led the people of Israel out of Egypt, crossing the Red Sea with dry feet."

"That was well before the Suez Canal," I said, chewing hard on a particularly tough piece of lamb because I didn't want to bite at the first lure.

"In your opinion, why did Moses, accompanied by his little tribe (a few hundred people at the very most) invent monotheism during that journey?" my mentor asked.

"Big question!"

Did this guy know I was transporting the Tablets of the Law, and was he trying to test me? I told myself *in petto* that he had been delegated by Rome and was perhaps supposed to come with me to get the stones out of Abyssinia. The merchandise was valuable enough to justify an army. I looked at him, smiling. He returned a complicitous smile. I relaxed and poured some more Chianti. I liked the idea of going to Djibouti with Rodriguez, who was sturdy, experienced, a bon vivant, and whose help could be invaluable to me.

"I think that Moses," I surprised myself by saying, "through his familiarity with Pharaoh, and knowing the complexity of relationships with Egyptian gods, had understood that there would be advantage in single control. It was really a question of power. A single God, a single intermediary; Moses made certain that his people would be under his thumb. When he received, or went to find, or invented the Tablets of the Law, Moses gave himself the legal framework he needed to control everything. The precepts are precise, but they invite different interpretations. He presented himself as God's spokesman. It was a stroke of genius."

"You don't believe," asked one of the fathers, "that these Tablets of the Law were dictated by God himself?"

"I have doubts, Father. The chosen people? Why this tribe on the shores of the Mediterranean in particular? Why would God have ignored the Indies and China? We accord great importance to monotheism because it suits us. It's an occidental idea."

"I'm always amazed to see that the great religions were

born in this land of sand and sun," said a third diner, the masturbator, who was clearly forgetting Buddhism.

I was into my fifth glass of Chianti and was pressing ahead: "That's what we call the essential triangle."

"You mean God in three persons?"

"No. That Christian invention is more Roman than Mosaic. The essential triangle, good fathers, is pig, woman, and money. To your health!"

The whole table began to look at me with embarrassment. Larochelle must be really exhausted, they were telling themselves, to be proffering such vulgarity.

"Explain yourself," Méridien demanded.

Out of the corner of my eye, I saw Rodriguez's face light up; he was quivering. He was even proud of me.

"I think if we analyze the laws that Moses brought down from the mountain where God had appeared to him in a cloud, we realize that these laws are interdictions. From the moment your people accept one God and reject idols, in order to lead them by the nose you have to multiply their interdictions precisely. To make myself clear, a summation goes like this: pig is not kosher, woman hides herself behind the veil, money is dirty. Judaism, Islam, Christianity. Whoever possesses the Tablets of the Law, Moses, Muhammed, or Jesus, holds an essential power over his people. But let us admit it, on a universal scale this remains a limited adventure."

"I find you very cynical," Méridien said.

"And I find him full of imagination," Rodriguez replied.

The good fathers poured themselves more cognac and I suspect that some of them slept poorly that night. There were other theological discussions. Was God a human invention or the reverse? Why not a pantheon of gods? Why is it that the One God of Moses triumphed over Venus and Zeus? Amen.

I went to the terrace to smoke a Silver Star from a package that was lying on the table. I smoke a cigarette a year; this one, made of good, pale, slightly sweet Ethiopian tobacco, burned gently under the stars. Rodriguez came and joined me.

"When are we leaving?" he asked.

I had guessed right. He was not in Harar by chance.

"The train leaves the city at three o'clock tomorrow, I would have liked to visit Harar, see Rimbaud's house. If we're at the station around one o'clock, we'll have the crate put on a platform car. I have all the papers but I hadn't foreseen needing a train ticket for you."

"I'll take care of it," he said, then went to talk to Méridien.

The night passed in a wink. The roosters began crowing at four o'clock, it was an outright competition rather than a concert, each gallinacean bent on having the tribe at his feet.

Breakfast with Canadian Jesuits is always an ode to the lumberjack menu. Bacon, fried eggs, potatoes, toast, baked beans, milk, jam, coffee. Communal life has its better moments.

A young teacher, Father Bertrand, a guy of my own age, took me into town on foot. We crossed through the market, which was already swarming with people at this early morning hour, and I bought a second knife with a brass-mounted horn handle, this for Rodriguez. The fruits and vegetables here at the Harar market seemed to me fresher than those in the capital. The citizens, on the other hand, looked more ragged. Father Bertrand told me quietly that a great deal of hashish was consumed in the region, it soothed the pangs of hunger and poverty. Rimbaud alluded to this, I thought I recalled, in his correspondence with his friend Izambert or with his family, I couldn't remember which. Yet I had read his writings avidly, learned his poems by heart, shuddered with horror at the story of his love affair with Verlaine who, one day in a hotel room, had shot and wounded him with a revolver. When Rimbaud stopped writing, he didn't do it by halves, he was an all-or-nothing guy. Verlaine had soured him on rhyming, he sought escape. He even enlisted in the Dutch colonial army, but deserted. If he had known the Company of Jesus, he would have made a magnificent recruit. He detested religiosity and priests, but was in search of the ultimate adventure.

"Do you think the city has changed much in a hundred years?"

I was asking this just in case, how could Father Bertrand possibly know?

"They tell me not. It has spread, the population has doubled, two or three barracks have gone up, but otherwise there's the same dust, the same sun, the same kind of people, the same crafts."

The women of Harar weave straw, dyed red and black, into baskets of various sizes — marvels.

> *Barefoot white hunter on the trot*
> *Through the Pasture panicky*
> *Could you not, should you not*
> *Know a little botany?*

These ironic lines sprang suddenly to my mind when I saw the plants being sold by the devotees of leaf medicine. All the women were chewing betel and spitting jets of red juice on the ground where we were walking.

"Rimbaud was our age when he arrived here," I said to Father Bertrand. "One's thirties bring the epiphany of all desires. Is there no one left who knew him?"

"Well," Bertrand replied, "there is one old woman who claims to be his daughter, but we have to cross through the old native city to find her."

He led me to where she was camped outside the former offices of the Bardy Company. It was from here that Arthur Rimbaud had left to explore the Ogaden, wishing to sell arms to Menelik, the uncle of Hailé Selassie. The poet had then ridden on horseback from Harar all the way to the Entoto Palace on Addis Ababa's heights. He had entered the Ghebbi, where I myself had been received. He too had bowed low to the Negus Negushi, but without obtaining a fair price for his merchandise. Did he know the Tablets of the Law lay sleeping a few hours from there? He wouldn't have given a damn: crap on laws, to hell with the tablets, religious claptrap! Rimbaud was into serious things: trade, arms, discovery of new lands where no white hunter had ever set foot.

The old woman was huddled and wrapped in an ageless grey cloth.

"That's Rimbaud's daughter," Bertrand whispered in my ear.

At thirty, Arthur set up house with a native woman, he betrayed Verlaine with a girl of the desert who was as exotic and artful as his verse. His daughter had no teeth left, her soft mouth made what she was saying impossible to understand. What was she singing to me? "Au clair de la lune"? For a few centimes would she have recited ... "Shopkeeper! Colonist! Medium! Your rhyme will spring, pink or white, like a ray of sodium, like a rubber swelling ...?" No, of course not, no lines, no memories. Mme Rimbaud of Harar, daughter of the poet of puberty, was born of old lovemaking sparked in Ogaden, well after the warm wind of poetry. She was, this old potato, the child of a leather and coffee merchant; her father Arthur had come around to making money, as any ordinary person does, to keep body and soul together.

The gloom that fell over me that morning! What had the world come to? He who used to transfigure my life with words and colours, who had nourished my years of happiness, had left on earth only these shapeless cells, this ailing old woman leaning against a concrete pillar, with a chipped plate at her feet and a cardboard sign on which I could read: "Two cents for the poets, A. R."

I emptied my pockets, left over one hundred thalers in the dish, my eyes were haggard, my heart ached, I tugged on Bertrand's sleeve and we left at a run for the Villa Manrèse. It did no good being a poet, it was better to be a Jesuit!

I had barely caught my breath at the villa when a telephone call was being announced for me. It was Véronik. She told me that Tafari had arrived in Germany and his exhibition was enjoying great success. She had also had occasion to talk to the Emperor who was not worried about the damage. But there was something else. She was afraid there was going to be trouble. I must redouble my vigilance because the Anti-quarian Brothers had learned of the disappearance of the tablets and were out to get their hands on them.

"They're professional thieves," she added, "but they don't know who you are, or even what train you've left by. They'll certainly be waiting at the station, though. His Majesty warned me that they're ready to pay a high price for the words of God. Be very careful!"

I was moved that Véronik still cared about me. I tried to

reassure her: "I'm not leaving alone, my comrade Rodriguez is here, I talked to you about him, he'll be going with me, don't worry. Thank you for calling me. You're marvellous!"

We kissed over the telephone, which was utterly ludicrous, all the more since our voices were practically drowned out by static on the line.

"What about Rimbaud?" she asked.

"Rimbaud left me his *Illuminations*. Don't expect more of him. His traces here are pathetic. My poem of Abyssinia is going to be you."

I remained by the telephone, as motionless as stone, Véronik's voice still in my ear. The Antiquarian Brothers? Were they talked about in my encyclopedias? I had to leave. Rodriguez was already waiting for me, we said our goodbyes to the soldiers of God and hurried away to the station. I found the crate as I'd left it, on a flatcar covered with arches of brown canvas, with a miscellany of objects piled all around, and a heap of mail bags against one side. Who could ever write as much as Arthur had to his mother long ago? I checked the cover of the crate, the seals were still in place.

The heat was torrid in the dust of the sorting yard where we stayed standing near the tracks, watching the train being made up. No Antiquarians on the horizon. Brakemen bustled about, steel jaws clamped over buffers, cars slammed together hard. Most of the workers were wearing incomplete uniforms, this one a jacket, that one a cap, either the railway company was scrimping or the railwaymen were selling their clothes an item at a time to go and drink in the brothels surrounding the station. This was where Rodriguez took me, after checking the time of departure, he had an urgent matter to attend to, an urge for a dancer perhaps. I sat at a low table and ordered a Pepsi-Cola while my master tumbled his mistress behind a red cotton curtain that fluttered in the breeze of an electric fan.

Once we were sitting side by side in the train, Rodriguez leaned on me and went to sleep. He was heavy. He snored so hard that the women in the car laughed, putting their hands over their mouths. Four soldiers had hung their guns on nails and were playing cards on an empty fuel can. I too closed my eyes, but without having sleep come. I was seeing Véronik's shoulders, I was hearing her voice tell me of her love. I was in rapture, I was enjoying a blissful insomnia. To have her closer to me, between the pages of a guide to East Africa published in Milan in 1938 (Mussolini had had his conquered territories mapped), I had slipped a eucalyptus leaf, whose fragrance I associated with our nights in Addis, and whose graceful shape reminded me of hers. If only I were Rimbaud himself recalling that scene!

The train was moving along at a good clip when Rodriguez opened his eyes at last. The track was following a steep incline, and he had slithered along the bench on his behind and very nearly fell off the end of it.

"Where are we?" he said anxiously, then recovered, massaged the gooseflesh on his cheeks, and asked for something to drink. All the windows were open and the air coming into the car seemed to me increasingly humid.

"We're getting near the Red Sea," he said. "Your Rimbaud first arrived in Aden, on the opposite side, it's hell there, like Djibouti, where we're going. It's so hot that when evening comes, the richest people drive back and forth in convertible cars on the only paved highway, behind the city, to catch some fresh air. What time do we arrive?"

"The timetable says midnight, but one never knows," I replied. "I must warn you, Rodriguez, that the Antiquarian Brothers are after us according to Véronik, without knowing who we are, though they know about our mission."

"Véronik's your girlfriend?"

I expected Rodriguez to slap his thighs and make fun of the situation. I was ready to laugh with him. Instead, his face turned serious and he asked: "Did Véronik tell you how they found out?"

"No," I said, "she saw the Emperor and reported. It was His Majesty, I think, who warned her."

"His Majesty is a little swindler!" Rodriguez snapped angrily. "He uses you to save the tablets, you succeed without setting off riots, you leave with the stones, you're the next thing to a new Moses, and all this time his aim has been to make sure he'll hold onto his power. He wanted the Ark of the Covenant to leave Abyssinia, where it's in danger, so as to get it back later, negotiating its return. He will use bribery. We're only conveyors, and for all I know, those four soldiers there at the end perhaps already consider us their prisoners. And you saw none of it!"

When I finally succeeded in getting in a word, I asked him why the Antiquarians frightened him so.

"They're pirates. Murderers. They've been buccaneering along the coast of Somalia forever, and delicacy is not their style, I can assure you."

What Rodriguez did not like, and what I finally understood, was that I had been just a convenience for His Majesty. By leading a foreigner, a white besides, to commit this theft, he could always wash his hands of me. For his relationship with the people, it was even a bold strategy. As a *farenghi*, I could only be an enemy. For my own part, I had not yet decided on the final destination for the tablets, but in my naïveté, I had believed I could dispose of them; that was even the most interesting challenge. If these stones had a magic power, as I had been told, I wanted them to serve some purpose. Rodriguez declared he was convinced that the Antiquarian Brothers had been tipped off by the Negus, who was going to buy the stones back from them.

"I found you a knife in the Harar market." I took it out of my backpack to give it to him.

"A knife? They'll sink it between our shoulder blades! What are we going to do?"

We had nearly four hours ahead of us, and Rodriguez began

to think, head between his hands, elbows firmly planted on his thighs. I didn't know the Antiquarians then, but today I still shudder when I see a refined shop window with a sign announcing: "Antiques Bought and Sold." The Somali pirates, they say, do not negotiate, they take, and when the gold or artifacts dug up by archaeologists are in short supply, they practise slavery, a sweep through a village, a forced march, the human cattle cross the Red Sea, and are sold at the market in Aden where rich Arabs aren't bothered by conscience.

"The Antiquarian Brothers don't know we're not armed," Rodriguez whispered finally, "that could play in our favour, but we'll have to move very fast."

If the Antiquarians were waiting at the station and spotted us, we'd have only one solution: grab the soldiers' guns and hold the fort until the army intervened. We'd have to fight hammer and tongs and be lucky because our Abyssinians' rifles clearly belonged with the shipment that Rimbaud delivered to Menelik.

Rodriguez said, "I'd be surprised if they dared cross the lines established by the border police. Djibouti is a French territory. They'll be waiting for us on the way out. In fact, they're not interested in us, it's the crate they're after. How did you identify it?"

"*Tables*."

"Seriously?!"

"Véronik and I thought the simplest was to be truthful." But note that we didn't add the name of the prophet!

"Well then, there's nothing we can do other than ask the protection of the governor."

Should I have been distrusting Rodriguez as I should have distrusted the Negus? Were they all trying to use me for their own ends? These are pertinent questions, but one is alone at this game, as I am this evening, sitting at a table in the pizzeria du Phare, the Lighthouse Pizzeria. Yesterday, I ate a restaurant called Le Chalut, the Dragnet. Tomorrow, it will be crepes or paella. But every time, I find myself sitting opposite an empty chair, without a male friend or a woman to talk to. I wasted an hour chatting up the hotel receptionist before finding out that she was married and the mother of two children. The more girls I cruise, the more mothers with children I find. How come they retire from the discotheque and dalliance circuit while they're still so enticing?

Not only am I alone, but no one is supposed to find out where I'm staying. To mix up my tracks, I took the bus to Bayonne, where I telephoned Rome this morning. I'm having the worst time concentrating as the deadline approaches, but I must stick to the plan and follow it like a robot. I gave the Superior General of the Jesuits a general delivery address at Lourdes to write to me. They'll certainly have it watched day and night, but they won't catch me. If I chose Lourdes, I explained to him, it's because the place is symbolic on two counts: first, my tablets are every bit as miraculous as the grotto water in which the faithful come to bathe; second, the business has all the necessary cash at its disposal. Collection boxes, artfully placed near all the underground basilica's exits, sales of millions of candles, alms deposited in woven baskets, rentals of mini cars for the sick, all this smells so fragrantly of money that Rome has only to send a cheque and Lourdes will pay me the desired mite in cash. I'm not accepting credit-card payment or even a draft on the Bank of the Holy Ghost. I've given enough emotionally, physically, and spiritually, they can do what they want with the tablets afterwards, add a pilgrimage, create a museum, bury them under Saint Peter's, negotiate a protocol of exchange with Israel — that will be the last of my worries.

"And if we don't pay you what you've asked," the Superior General of the Jesuits dared hiss into the receiver, "what are you going to do with the tablets?"

"Have a picnic."

I don't like threats. Rather than threaten, I suggested he think more about the Commandments, remember what was graven in the stone from Mount Sinai:

Thou shalt have no other Gods before me.
Thou shalt not make any graven image, nor any likeness.
Thou shalt not bow down before idols.
Keep the Sabbath day to sanctify it.
Honour thy father and thy mother that thy days
    may be long in the land.

The Superior General interrupted me.

"This isn't exegesis, Larochelle, we're dealing with basics. I know what follows, on killing, adultery, stealing, bearing false witness, the neighbour's wife. If what I'm told is founded, you have little respect yourself for the Lord's Commandments."

"I don't offer myself as a model, General," I replied. "If you refuse to buy the tablets, it's the Church that's going to be the poorer for it."

What the Jesuits detest more than all else is a recalcitrant soldier. They'll quickly isolate him, put him in solitary. Knowing this, I've isolated myself inside the luxurious walls of Eugénie's palace. The sea keeps me company, she's fickle but always present, with mauves and oranges bathing ocean liners in the distance. At night, I imagine New York out there, opposite, bathed by the same salt water. Oh, when shall I see my North America again?

8

THE AFRICAN NIGHT, DEEP AND disquieting, cloaked the arid hills in purple, signalling our approach to the shores of the Red Sea. The clickety-clack of the wheels on the rails smothered the cries of nocturnal animals.

I was sweating heavily as I imagined our arrival in Somalia as worse than a season in hell, with accompaniment by an end-of-the-world orchestra. I could hear the impact of bullets smashing like ripe fruits. I saw the sweat and blood on our faces painting warrior masks. A breathless dash, a leap to the side, a ringing gunshot, an Antiquarian dropping before my eyes. The three Somalis had surely arrived before eleven o'clock; they had parked their Jeep mounted with an anti-tank gun on the south side of the station. Their first objective, attack the locomotive before it stopped. An armour-piercing shell placed squarely in the boiler, and the monster was exploding; in the confusion, Rodriguez and I ran along the track among wounded railway workers and dying passengers. Firemen were breaking open cars in flames, the Antiquarians were launching a flare that turned the apocalypse into the Fourth of July. The tablets' box had turned over without breaking open in the last car, where the bags of mail were burning, the flames licking at the tarpaulins, and the smoke giving us cover. Blindly, I was shooting all the bullets I'd filched from one of the Ethiopian guards. The antique Mauser was popping off like a Chinese cannon, bruising my shoulder; the Antiquarians were returning fire. Rodriguez was howling at the moon. It was a vision straight out of an American movie. Too many dead bodies, too much powder, napalm, and dust in the night.

We could certainly do better than imagine the worst. Which was why, as soon as the train arrived at Djibouti station, we jumped onto the platform, raced to the first uniformed figure, and claimed political asylum before any confrontation could arise.

"We declare ourselves prisoners and ask to see the governor," said Rodriguez to the station master, who blew three times on his nickel-plated whistle to call the border police, to whom we submitted our Canadian passports. The officers respectfully took our gold-stamped, overseas-blue, hardcover-bound documents, examined our faces and our photographs, repeated our names like a litany, checked in their big book of rules for the procedure to be followed when travellers declare themselves prisoners. It was a major event, a first at Djibouti station.

Midnight sounded. Then half past midnight. We knew it was not a convenient hour to visit the governor. Rodriguez suggested a solution: "Don't disturb anyone, put us in a cell with our baggage. We'll only open the box in the presence of the authorities. You can consult with your superiors tomorrow morning. We're calling for your protection."

A small troop of legionnaires surrounded us. Four porters slid the crate onto a red trolley, and the convoy set off for the prison, beyond doubt watched incredulously by the Antiquarians come to wait for us. Ironic parade, brilliant strategy. I was filled with admiration for the way in which my teacher was turning problems to our advantage.

Even in the middle of the night, the heat of Djibouti was crushing, and with sweat rising to our temples, we crossed Place Henri IV, where we saluted a statue of Joan of Arc holding an operetta-type lance, then gingerly walked through lanes leading to the warehouse district. The old yellow prison stood out in the darkness; rococo in style, it bore gashes in its pediment that had never been repaired.

Our arrival was unexpected. The prison director, wakened by the noise, informed us that one wing was occupied by petty criminals, that the real criminals were on an island farther north. He decided to lock us up in an unused part, had the crate placed in one cell, and offered us two others for the night. Mine was not a paragon of cleanliness but, situated on the ground floor, it turned out to be cool and pleasant, even if I was sharing my bed with a couple of dozen tiny creatures.

I went to sleep quickly. It's one of my secrets. I am refreshed abundantly. Even lying on stones, on the tarmac of a high-way, on a steel ship's deck, or curled up on this shoddy mattress that to me was as comfortable as the big bed at the Imperial Ghion. Where was Véronik sleeping that night? Why, between duty and love, had I chosen obedience? I was becoming bitter.

In the morning, over coffee, for which the prison director had invited us to his office, Rodriguez complained of not having slept a wink because he felt responsible for our cargo, and insisted on seeing the governor before noon. He was yawning, his beard was stubbly, his eyes red.

The governor's palace was only two kilometres from there, on a height of land; it had been built in the same period as the prison, was the same sandy colour, of the same colonial-military style. Three floors, big verandas on the north side, the French coat of arms above the main doors, which were flanked by two tricolour flags. The palace staff were in a flurry of excitement, the chief protocol officer was in charge of decorations for the annual grand ball preceding the summer holidays. Streamers were twisting in the wind, multicoloured balloons had been tied to the coconut and banana trees, making fairground posts of the trees. That very evening, we were told, the *Jean-Laborde*, twenty thousand tons, a hundred passengers, was arriving from Madagascar with the Minister of Foreign Affairs aboard. A great party was ahead, and for us, Rodriguez murmured in my ear, an incredible opportunity.

The governor, Monsieur Charles de Hautefleur, received us with a ready hand and a smile on his lips. He was a man in his fifties, dapperly dressed, visibly determined to turn a thankless chore in too hot a country into continuous pleasure. Even the size of his office was impressive, it was furnished with Louis XVI tables and armchairs, and had astonishing gilt decoration on the walls and at the corners of the ceiling. Monsieur de Hautefleur began with apologies for making us spend the night in obscurity, which, he quickly added with a laugh, in this torrid country was better anyway than spending it in the sun. Then he gathered his eighty kilos behind his desk, crossed his arms, checked to see if the fan over his head was turning fast enough, and invited us with his eyes closed to tell him our story.

Rodriguez played the humble card. He explained that we were two Jesuits in Abyssinia who had been induced, under duress, in the face of the dangers of revolution brewing there in the mountains of Addis, to try to protect some old Coptic relics. Then he turned the floor over to me. It was my turn and I must improvise. The governor seemed to be intelligent, and a French patriot; why not stroke him in the right direction?

"We thought, Your Excellency," I declared, "that these relics, old stones on which are said to be graven the words of God to Moses, ought to be examined scientifically. I can see no country other than France to succeed with such a study. You can call on eminent linguists and learned historians but, better still, I believe that we should bring these stones to the Louvre so that your experts can examine them in laboratory conditions. If they turn out to be authentic antiquities, I would not be surprised to see the Louvre devote a gallery to them."

The governor was salivating. I had him in my hand. Rodriguez didn't get what I was up to, not knowing how far I was going in my fabulation. Monsieur de Hautefleur, at this moment of intellectual pleasure, was unfortunately interrupted by the chief protocol officer, who was being punctilious over order, good taste, and hierarchy. The governor begged us to excuse him for a moment and concentrated on more urgent problems than ours: was the ship's captain going to be seated at Monsieur the Governor's table? Would the garrison commander be to the left of the minister's wife? Should a snack be prepared for the children? Was the 1740 gold and vermeil flatware to be used, or the silver purchased from Queen Victoria? Monsieur de Hautefleur took the opportunity to notify the chief protocol officer that places for us should be included at the banquet and the ball.

"You dance in spite of your vows?" he asked, a mite provocatively and with a hint of layman's prejudice.

I hastened to assure him: "We are, like all Jesuits, monsieur, men of the world."

If I had had time, I would have told him the saga of the new Company, the one the pope re-established in 1814 after abolishing the old one, which was accused of fraudulence and conspiracy. How many stories and evenings we might have devoted to our adventures in the old and new world! But my problem was not of historical nature.

"You were talking about the laboratories at the Louvre in Paris," de Hautefleur continued, liberating his employee and offering us a coffee or a lemonade.

With a cup in my hand, which was trembling a little with the enormity of the situation, I fired my best left hook at the governor.

"Monsieur de Hautefleur, Your Excellency, I was going to say that while we know how to dance, and we thank you for inviting us to your festivities, we are nevertheless, because we are members of an egalitarian company in the eyes of Jesus, committed to the strictest humility. I therefore propose that it be you, monsieur, who will have Moses's Tablets delivered to the Louvre, hoping that the grateful museum will give your name to the gallery in which they will be displayed. You are a senior official of the Republic on foreign posting; coming from you, this gift from God will receive the necessary attention, and you yourself will perhaps merit a certain esteem."

I didn't know if Rodriguez was following me, but I thought my little plan was rather nicely worked out. I was safeguarding the tablets, putting them under the protection of the French police, I was delivering them to a responsible institution, and I was offering to go with them so as not to lose sight of them. The cost of transporting them would be borne by the French government, moreover. As for how to get them back once they were in Paris, I had confidence in us. The agreement was sealed with a hearty handshake and a brimful glass of cognac after a last coffee.

"Cheers!" declared the mandarin.

On the way back to prison, in the blinding sunshine of midday, Rodriguez, laughing, was about to tell me what had been going through his mind when suddenly, this time, there was a burst of real live fire. Djibouti was literally shimmering with light, the bare walls of the warehouses reflected the heat, there was no one in sight, but rifle bullets were ricocheting off the concrete all around, tearing out chunks as big as my hand. A first legionnaire dropped, the others knelt and tried to return fire, Father Rodriguez suddenly doubled up as if trying to roll over, but let out a cry so loud that I threw myself face down in the dust. My teacher was hit. I crawled to his side. The shooters were hiding on the roofs. We could see them now, for an eternity there was a deafening exchange, one of the attackers fell into the street, then there was silence, the more surprising because it was sudden.

We counted our dead, two soldiers and my teacher who was dying, a brown stain on his back, blood in his mouth, he was gurgling. I said a prayer just in case, the legionnaires were perhaps Muslims but in these extreme situations the great religions accept compromises. The captain was wounded with a bullet in his thigh. An attacker lay farther off, his neck broken. Four victims. The Antiquarian Brothers, realizing they were not going to get their hands on the tablets, had decided to make us pay for their failure. It was an exorbitant price.

In the furnace-like street, I began to tremble, a delayed reaction, half-blinded by the white light, my shoulders shaken by a curious muscular reflex. Rodriguez was dying. Were we going to transport him, was there still a chance of saving him?

"A doctor! A doctor!" I shouted.

But no ambulance and no doctor came. Rodriguez expelled one last blood-filled spew, then jerked his head back against the asphalt and died without saying a word. I was alone again. I had lost one of the few men I respected in the Company. I had an intense desire to get drunk on whisky, like a cowboy, standing at the bar of a saloon, glass after glass until I too collapsed, with a perforated stomach.

The wounded captain sent one of his men to the prison for reinforcements. The man came back with ten soldiers and a truck. With the dead laid on the floor of the truck, we entered the courtyard of the institution in funeral-procession style. The director was surprised at the savagery of the attack on us.

"What are you transporting that's so valuable?" he asked.

I told him only the governor could explain. He lost no time telephoning the palace, I don't know what they may have told him but he was remarkably deferent subsequently, and, after ordering coffins, told me that we would bury Rodriguez in the little Catholic cemetery that very afternoon. The heat was such that I made no objection.

Under the shower in the prison director's quarters, from which warm water trickled parsimoniously, I soaped myself with a bar of Marseille and scrubbed with a horse-hair bath glove. I washed my sand- and blood-soiled clothes, which I laid out to dry on the parapet, and then went to lie down in my cell. I was dead tired. In a matter of minutes, a man had passed from life to death. I could very well have finished the same way, in the street, hopes and plans ruined by an avenging projectile.

Rodriguez had taken part of my life with him. All the adventures we had shared, all the places we had been together, who could I share these memories with now? With Rodriguez gone, I was left with the burden of our collective memory and all the advice he had lavished on me as my share of his legacy. Certainly, chance had smiled on me this time.

How much longer? Moving about as I had been doing for the past ten years, I had always felt I was defying destiny, but if destiny had been waiting for Rodriguez in Djibouti, Somalia, might it be waiting for me at the next stop? In Marseille?

The burial was restrained, in the shade of dwarf palm trees and stunted cypresses. The rows of the cemetery, rectangular and well-raked, were surrounded by a hedge of spiny bushes to keep out hyenas. When the legionnaires let go of the ropes holding Rodriguez's coffin, I felt a cry well up in me that I held back till the pain was piercing my sides and chest. I had never wept, even on the morning my mother had left home, and I was not going to shed tears over Rodriguez, any more than I had over leaving my Abyssinian princess. What's the point of tears that, with time, always dry in the end?

I was almost thirty-five, the age of the third novitiate's solemn vows, but I had given enough. The Company of Jesus could get along without me, I thought, and likewise our friends the Americans. Being in the Intelligence Service, I said to myself, consists of not farting around all one's life. I had served enough. I decided to withdraw from the world, *reductio*, retire to pleasant circumstances, I wanted to disappear in style. I needed money, a lot of money. I knew only one wicket at which to ask for my severance bonus — the one at la Banca de Sancti Spiritu. I took this decision very deliberately, while the sand was bouncing on the coffin cover, and I swore on the grave of my friend that I would not change my mind.

At nine o'clock that same night, the director of the institution and I left in a state-provided limousine preceded by two Jeeps and followed by two more. I learned then that the authorities, through the body of the slain Antiquarian, had identified the family of murderous brothers. They were already being hunted and would not survive very long. The legionnaires had not appreciated the ruckus and were counting on taking revenge for their dead.

In a few hours, I had transformed myself. From funeral to governor's ball, from man of duty to one who henceforth would think of his pleasure, there was a world of difference I decided to cross over to with vigour. In reality, still today when I walk on the blue carpeting of the Hôtel du Palais, along corridors hung with views of Biarritz and portrait photographs of celebrated and self-satisfied crowned heads, I wonder still how one gets to practice selfishness. I was brought up by an encyclopedist to believe that the human tribe needed guardians. That I should risk my life on occasion to avert mass slaughter. I was taught to fight against evil. It's not easy to abandon my human brothers to their wretched fate.

Amid the sound of the waves along the beach, I repeat aloud that the sign from heaven will come from Rome: "You made an honest offer, it's for them to react intelligently."

Tomorrow, I'll rent a car and be off to Lourdes to see if there's some satisfactory reply waiting at the post office; it's time I stirred a bit outside this room, where every day I've been writing something that will serve no purpose if Moses comes out the winner of this contest.

9

GOVERNOR DE HAUTEFLEUR COULD NOT resist announcing to his minister that he was making a gift of the tablets to France. The minister haughtily looked him up and down. Surely it was his own rightful place to repatriate these treasures. The tour he had undertaken amid the sound and fury of decolonization had proven to be gloomy and negative, but if he was bringing the tablets to Paris on his return, he could call a press conference and much admiration could redound to him (he would mention de Hautefleur's name, of course). What a magnificent gift he was being handed! He gave a little gasp or two of pleasure. Moses's Tablets! He wanted to meet the Jesuit who had given them to France.

I was sitting in the right-hand corner of the ballroom with the ladies and gentlemen of Djibouti's bourgeoisie, who were gossiping as only colonials can. The prison director had lent me a uniform that gave me the appearance of a foreign legion officer in a 1950s American movie; a small moustache would have looked well on me, I thought. I was still contemplating my new life plan when I was summoned to come and meet the bigwigs.

The minister was very civilized, he made a point of expressing his sympathy and that of his government; he had learned of the tragic death of my companion-in-arms.

"He was a brave man," said the governor, "I was able to judge his character even though we were acquainted only a few hours. I have ordered a tombstone engraved," he added, "to recall that Father Rodriguez died for France."

Died for France! I succeeded in suppressing a smile, which changed on my lips to a grimace.

The minister introduced me to the people of his retinue, his secretary would take me under his wing the next day, I must ab-so-lute-ly board the *Jean-Laborde* with the tablets and accompany the embassy to the City of Light. He introduced me to his wife and to his daughter, who was sitting, meekly and resigned to boredom, between two bearded and bemedalled gentlemen.

The orchestra struck up a foxtrot, the governor rose to open the ball, the minister held out his arm to his wife, and I bent toward Marie-Louise de Bonchâteau. I was telling myself that Rodriguez would have wanted me to enjoy myself, forget the wound of his passing. I requested the honour of having

Mademoiselle Bonchâteau dance with me.

"Good for you! You're choosing life, Father!" the minister declared as he moved onto the waxed dance floor.

Marie-Louise had moist hands and agile feet. She was spirited and displayed her twentysomething years and the confident manner that sets Parisian women apart from others.

"Protocol would have had me dance with my neighbour, a distinguished member of the Académie française, and I must thank you for rescuing me from his tobacco-smelling breath. He chews!"

I don't know how many Djibouti ladies blanched with jealousy watching the two of us dance, our arms around each other; the colony's elegant set gradually joined the dance and finally we could talk, heads slightly bent, hips following the rhythms of a loud, multi-hued orchestra.

"So you're coming with us for the last leg of the journey? What are these tablets my papa has talked about?" the young woman asked.

"The Tablets of the Law that govern Occidental morality," I replied simply. "They're going to be deposited in the Louvre."

"The real tablets?!"

"We shall see. That's what the Ethiopians believe. Is it a legend or the truth? You know that these questions are never settled."

The foxtrot became a twist, which didn't facilitate our conversation. I was hot in my military tie and my sword belt was hanging crooked.

"There was talk of a skirmish," she said, moving fists and feet.

I told her how we had been savagely attacked and that same afternoon I had buried a very dear friend.

"And you're dancing now!" Marie-Louise looked aghast. "That's a very strange way to mourn! Aren't you a priest?" She was very serious all of a sudden.

"There are two ways to flee from battle," I said to her. "Forwards or backwards; in the first case, you get a bullet in the back, in the second, you get it in the forehead. I've chosen this way, I'm defying death by dancing as best I can."

Marie-Louise laughed heartily; her father, watching us from the corner of his eye, seemed reassured, the young people were having fun, he could go back to the affairs of state that were preferably discussed between several good bottles brought up from the governor's cellar.

When the orchestra regained its breath, a slightly pedantic little shrimp of a man came and cut in, his name was at the top of the list in Mademoiselle Bonchâteau's dance program, I bowed as was proper and went to the balcony overlooking the garden beside a terrace crammed with gigantic ferns. It was hot and humid, and my shirt was sopping with sweat. Perching on the low wall, I looked back into the ballroom, Marie-Louise had already changed partner; she was duty-bound to be constantly playing the minister's daughter. Couldn't she even give a little ginger to a young career?

I closed my eyes, the music became softer, a waltz struck

up, and I began to run toward Véronik, who was whirling about on the screen of my brain. Could I reproach her for sacrificing her own happiness for the happiness of others, I who had offered up ten years of my life on the altar of the Company? What was sticking in my throat most of all was the double cross the Negus had pulled on us. That adventure had left me two bereavements, the one of love and the one of friendship.

This was where I was in my reasoning, with some erotic images in my mind straight out of the Ghion album. I wasn't feeling much pride, and a Jesuit without pride is a beaten Jesuit, *ipse dixit* Maximilian Ryllo. Why did I think of Ryllo, the Polish father who, after a detour through Syria, had become rector of the college of the propaganda at Malta? He had been one of Rodriguez's favourite characters. The Jesuit Ryllo, who spoke several oriental languages, one day disguised himself as a sultan in robe and turban to go into Egypt, and then, dressed as an Armenian merchant, turned up in Khartoum where he perhaps crossed paths with Rimbaud, before dying a wretched death of cholera, at forty. Rodriguez used to quote him as an example, stressing the necessity of assuming the colour of the walls for survival. He had himself followed Ryllo's footsteps when leaving Cairo, which hadn't stopped him losing his bet over a bullet that had pierced his spine, then pulverized his duodenal bulb. Ryllo and Rodriguez had both died when they were barely past forty! I looked up at the sky. Several planets were awaiting me. A spaceship would be welcome. I longed to eat up my silken ties, my vows, like a chrysalis. And live!

When I opened my eyes, Marie-Louise was standing before me, a glass of champagne in each hand, a smile lighting her face.

"I didn't want to interrupt your thoughts," she said, handing me one of the glasses. "I was sure it was your body I was looking at, but you seemed to be somewhere else, as if your mind had left it here, or rather, as if you yourself were off exploring the mountains of Abyssinia."

"Well," I replied, getting to my feet, "let's celebrate my return and your arrival!"

The champagne glasses clinked, and we swilled the bubbles of the cold wine, which sparkled like the curiosity in the girl's eyes.

"Was she very beautiful?" she asked.

"Who do you mean?" I said, astonished.

"The lady of the tablets."

This chick had some damn intuition!

"Let's not talk about it anymore," I said. "And take me dancing, only music can console me."

But she was insistent.

"Tell me about your adventures instead. Let's listen to the orchestra from here, I've had enough of being made dizzy."

"You're being very serious. What do you do in life when you're not going on trips with your father? Are you studying?"

Marie-Louise was completing a *licence* in literature, and felt drawn to psychoanalysis. We talked about books we had both read — Gide, Sartre, Camus. Perhaps I even stooped to recounting several anecdotes experienced in the tropics, where I had never set foot. Talking was doing both of us a great deal of good, and I felt a friendship forming, which is rare between a man and a woman. I didn't want her to think me indifferent to her charms, but we agreed tacitly, in the circumstances, to further explore our future without yielding to bodily urges. What a Jesuit! I thought, then turned seriously to the game at hand.

At the end of the night, when the minister and the governor and his retinue retired and all that remained in the big ballroom were limp decorations, empty glasses, and tipsy night owls, Marie-Louise left me, planting on my cheek the kiss of a little sister hoping to console me. It was soft and warm like candle wax. We each went our own way in the dawning but already bright light of a sun that was preparing to beat upon the slack sea with all its might.

On the way back to the barracks, escorted by my legionnaires who had downed a glass or two and slept near the conveniences, I had a moment of distress. I was imagining life in Djibouti, on the threshold of boredom, which only balls at the governor's palace could relieve. Domesticity in Djibouti! Any time I thought about retiring, the nomad in me would get restless. We were marching military fashion, I was remembering a song by Prévert and Montand.

Back at the prison, I didn't sleep much. I would close my eyes, then when I felt the heat stifling me, I would splash myself with tepid water from a bucket and lie naked under the fan in the deserted corridor until it all evaporated, which created a pleasantly cool feeling that was as factitious as fleeting.

Around midday, some baggage handlers and several coolies came to fetch the crate and put it on board the ship. I insisted on following the operation, fearing the worst, which did not happen. We met up with no Antiquarian murderers or outraged Ethiopians. The dockers worked well; with a block and pulleys and their taut muscles, they hoisted the tablets to the first deck, where a flap door opened wide enough to swallow the work of Moses. Joining the minister's baggage in the hold, the blond wood crate, surrounded by large, supple leather suitcases and rattan baskets, was going to have a pleasant trip.

The minister's secretary had managed well, I was given a cabin with a porthole overlooking the water, the whole decor nicely done in fine woods with brass nails around a small bed chained to the steel wall; I was keeping company with the upper crust of the upper deck, steps away from the suite occupied by Marie-Louise and her mother. The five days of the voyage were five picture-postcard days. An eclectic crowd was sailing aboard the *Jean-Laborde*: aid workers going home with bushy beards and Marxist chatter; schoolteachers on holiday from the colonies in mini-bikinis, hormones skin deep; noisy children never willing to leave the swimming pool; and then, exotic summum, at the far end of the big lounge, where the window curtains had all been closed at his insistence, Timothy Leary himself, in cast-Indian dress, small bells around his neck, who was returning from a speaking tour on the psychedelic revolution, of which he was apostle to the world. The American was surrounded by emaciated young people floating between two states of consciousness and tapping on tambourines.

On the second day, while gazing at tiny fishing ports on the horizon, where medieval boats rode sleepily at anchor in the evening mist, while deciding whether to play canasta or count the dolphins that were following the *Jean-Laborde* for the pleasure of the table scraps the kitchen staff was hurling overboard, I announced to Marie-Louise that I was going to approach the famous guru.

"What are you going to ask him?" she enquired, a mite possessively, as if I could discuss things only in her company.

"Leary knows a lot about the Orient, about Zen, and about drugs," I told her. "He's not a Cartesian. I'd like to know what he thinks of what I'm doing."

"He'll laugh in your face. I'd watch my step if I were you."

"I'm not going to tell him he's travelling with the Ark

of the Covenant! I talked to you yesterday about the art of mental restriction. Trust me. I want to test his brain power."

I entered the holy of holies. The contrast between the bright light of day and the artificial twilight of the lounge made me blink.

"Come in, come in!" called the guru.

After the customary kowtowing and opening pleasantries, I informed the author that I wished to consult him on a book I was writing.

"And what might that be?" he asked.

"A work on the Ten Commandments for the Company of Jesus."

"You're a Jesuit?" Leary made an admiring O with his lips as he lifted a marijuana cigarette to them.

"Not for long," I said softly.

He nodded, took my hands in his and said firmly: "Father, I know of only one way of approaching God, and that's through LSD. Have you tried the trip?"

"Mister Leary, the *Jean-Laborde* is enough for me, I have no need to undertake a chemical voyage, believe me."

"You're wrong!" And he let go of my hands.

"Do you consider the Ten Commandments still to be relevant in modern society?"

The guru shifted position, he had a cramp in his left calf muscle, rearranged some cushions, and fixed me with a most intense stare. Deep in his eyes, I could see the waves of the Pacific breaking on the rocks of Big Sur.

"The sixties are going to make a clean sweep," he declared with a swing of his arms, he was wearing black running shoes under his cotton skirts. "We're approaching the shores of humanity's greatest revolution since the Middle Ages. Psychedelic drugs are enabling us to explore hitherto unused capacities of our brains. The Ten Commandments don't mean much anymore. The sexual revolution is going to change relationships between women and men, it's going to leave God's dictates far behind. Psychoanalysis has already disrupted our prejudices, LSD is going to transform life. Look at me!"

I looked at him. He was swelling up. I sensed his mind vacillating.

"I was just another philosophy professor at a state university, now I'm the new Moses, and I can tell you that the Ten Commandments are going to be replaced by just one: 'Turn on, tune in, drop out.'"

Then he lay back softly against the silk cushions, swallowing a pink pill administered by a hippie girl the way communion is given in our churches. I tiptoed away, convinced that the tablets were antiquities henceforth.

A bit later, in the afternoon, leaning on a lifeboat turned upside down on the deck, I recounted my conversation to Marie-Louise. We chatted decorously as friends, although, enticed by the scent of suntan lotion, I did feel a small hollow inside, a slight desire to remove her flowered bikini, but she consistently kept her distance, as measured by her mother in her role as chaperone. I didn't push.

There had to be danger for her to spread her thighs. We were halfway through the Suez Canal, the ship was moving slowly, the propellers turning gently, the silent vessel gliding between the canal walls like a heavy sleigh. On either side of the *Jean-Laborde*, as far as the eye could see, desert, a few palm trees, caravans, whose camel drivers paid us no attention, all breathtakingly beautiful and calm. I was holding Marie-Louise by the arm, we were leaning on the railing in the shadow of a lifeboat on its davits when, in the midst of the torpor reigning over the passengers, a sudden noise shook the air, as if the steel hull were tearing on some spur. The ship began to tremble with increasing violence, sailors ran this way and that, the loudspeaker barked orders, panic took hold of everyone, sirens wailed, some people flattened themselves against the deck bulkheads, others ran for the lifebuoys, a fat little man armed with a safety axe was running in all directions, furiously chopping at all the deck chairs he came across; I took Marie-Louise to my cabin, undressed her, slipped with her under the shower, then we curled up on the little bed where we made love as if it was the last time before the end of the world. Between our kisses she didn't lose her head, I groped for her sex, she kept crying:

"Is the ship going to sink?"

I was the one who was sinking — our thighs were shiny with semen and we were gasping for breath. Then the ship calmed as did our lovemaking, smiles returned, we'd crossed the Rubicon.

That evening at the captain's table, there was no shortage of speculation. What had caused that shaking halfway through the canal? Why the distress signals in the middle of the day, had the ship been damaged? I watched Marie-Louise closely, but she picked at her salad like a minister's daughter. The engineer declared that we had hit the carcass of a tank, plane, or small ship sent to the bottom during the war launched by the English and French in collusion with Israel against the Egyptians. But the canal had been cleaned up, hadn't it? One of the three propellers had been damaged, said the engineer, the authorities would have to be notified that the keel of the *Jean-Laborde* had grated over a memento of war, we had been fortunate not to have sunk. These gentlemen were just conjecturing. I was the only one who knew what had really happened.

When the time came for after-dinner cognacs, I took Marie-Louise aside and told her the truth, I owed her that.

"When the ship began to jolt about, we were opposite Mount Sinai," I told her, "at the fifteen-kilometre point. You could have drawn a straight line from the canal into the plain where Moses came down from the mountain with the words of God in his arms. The tablets remembered. They wanted to leave their tabernacle and go back to the land of Israel. The prophets predicted the end of time, you know, the day when these stones would return to the soil they came from. The night will replace the day, the stars will pale, the light of the sun and the moon will go out, great whirlwinds of sand will lift the houses, and all life will cease on earth, for God will take back his words and the stones will crumble. I knew there would be a divine manifestation when the tablets passed, but I didn't know what form Yahweh's anger would take."

"And you thought of making love to soothe the Creator!" Marie-Louise exclaimed, not sure whether to laugh or be lost in admiration.

"Don't say a word of it to the engineer, he wouldn't understand a thing about the spiritual dimension of this," I said with a smile.

"Do you really think we were part of a miracle?"

"A Jesuit can't lie," I told her before swallowing the last mouthful of cognac from the bottom of my glass.

Marie-Louise was neither naive nor gullible, but she would not forget our encounter with divinity.

Today, I'm hurtling toward Lourdes in a small, red, rented Lancia, with polished steel hubcaps, its open roof letting in the light and the warm wind of the Basque countryside. I'm hoping to find an intelligent reply from my superiors. I haven't gambled my life for peanuts, and most of all, I haven't liked being manipulated by the Emperor. How much did Rome's diplomats know? If they were ready to sacrifice Rodriguez, what had the King of kings promised them?

"Gentlemen, if you wish to recover the texts of Moses and continue to insist that there is only one God, you will write me a little note of thanks accompanied by a bank draft for ten million American dollars. It's not much to pay for the divine words. It won't ever erase the memory of Véronik, but will apply a touch of balm to my aching heart."

This was the kind of language I used. I stressed the Church's loss of prestige in recent years, I recalled that the Temple veil could still be torn. If my superior did not feel authorized, I added, he had only to consult the sovereign pontiff, who would certainly be able to ante up this little golden package.

The city of Lourdes is rich and, with the addition of Moses's Tablets, the sum advanced will be reimbursed in two years by the flow of pilgrims. Already, since I slipped my treasure in its sacred wrappings under the stairs of the ancient basilica, the rate of miracles has jumped dramatically. The newspapers are saying that not a single paralytic leaves Lourdes on crutches. The crowds are getting denser, their faith is palpable almost, divine effluvia have pervaded the air, and the candles are burning brighter than ever before.

I had a stroke of luck — between the basilica and the grotto where Mary appeared, I found a hideaway for the tablets. It's an old gardener's shed where hoes and shovels used to be kept, but Lourdes has mechanized, and no one ever comes anymore to open the steel door; I'm the one now who has its key.

I review my strategy with pride as the highway slips away at top speed under the car, but I can't help thinking with anger of what will have to happen if what I'm asking for is turned down. I'll do something terrible, I've indicated to my former leaders, I'll shake the throne of Saint Peter!

10

THE PORT OF MARSEILLES, FROM the dazzling-white railings of the *Jean-Laborde*, offered an industrial landscape amid a forest of cranes. We were a long way from the boulevard called La Canebière and from maritime pines, no white heath or spindle trees or chalk cliffs on the horizon, only containers piled up on the docks, and, in the distance, waving his arm, Marie-Louise's fiancé, looking like an abandoned elf. He was a young École polytechnique graduate madly in love with the minister's daughter. Once we were off the boat, Marie-Louise hastened to introduce me to him: "This is Father Larochelle, who looked after us during the crossing. I learned a lot about the Company of Jesus. He was catechising me for several days, too."

"Oh," replied the fiancé, "I'd be so happy to stand beside you at the baptismal fonts, dearest!"

What an asshole! I mean, in this day and age! But Marie-Louise had already rediscovered virginity and put our excitement out of mind. She talked about the coasts of Sardinia and the extraordinary calm of the Mediterranean.

"It was a fine voyage," I confirmed. "I would have liked it to last forever, we could have sailed as far as China, where our Jesuit fathers served the rulers in Peking several centuries ago."

"Father Larochelle talked international politics with Papa, darling; and he's a marvellous pianist who played Bach or Trenet on request ..."

Marie-Louise was positively cooing.

"The mists from morning on were laden with smells of the sea ..."

I took my leave of the Polytechnique graduate and his Parisian maiden; I still had things to do, and for the Company of Jesus I still had a mission to accomplish. Rodriguez's death, which had certainly been reported in refectories the world over, could only confer a hero's stature on me. The bank accounts of foreign missions would be available for a few weeks yet. I had the means to do what I wanted. No point worrying the authorities before the time came, no one knew my intentions yet.

We had agreed, through the secretary and his assistants, to meet again in Paris the evening of the following day. A customs official authorized by the minister was to accompany me with the tablets. The goodbyes were brief and heartfelt, particularly since they were not final.

The train trip from Marseilles to the Gare de Lyon in Paris was exhausting. The customs man ate garlic sausage, cutting it with his Laguiole knife, without uttering a word. I had nothing to read. To keep myself busy, I jotted down the various strategies that had got me this far, which I would summarize as follows: semblance of innocence, fast footwork, mental restriction, and Houdini-style disappearance at the right moment.

The minister's press conference at the Louvre, in the Egyptian Room on the first floor, was a huge success. The exotic finger food heaped on the central table had been polished off in four minutes by the herd of journalists and diplomatic and political guests. There was no one in the diplomatic corps representing the Emperor, his ambassador having just been called home, Hailé Selassie was assembling his loyal supporters. This gave me the opportunity to explain that the chaotic situation in Abyssinia justified the safeguarding of Moses's Tablets. The young revolutionaries, for their part, were not going to bring the scorn of Moscow down on their heads by demanding the return of religious relics!

The relics had been unpacked, and in a kind of studied negligence were displayed in their scented wrappings on a pedestal with, in the background, pharaohs' mummies, brazen serpents, idols, and frescos the like of which Moses had known before the flight from Egypt. It was a scene of grandeur, photographers buzzed about like flies, the lighting for television illuminated everything so intensely that one might have imagined a brief appearance by Yahweh himself. If he had been invited, God would have congratulated the minister on his initiative, thanked the eldest daughter of the church for preserving the proof that there is but one God, and joined the guests in drinking a champagne toast.

A journalist from *La Croix* wanted to know if it wasn't dangerous to put the tablets in proximity to impious works.

"God is explicit in his Commandments, he abhors idols," he insisted.

"You're right," I told him (this was the only thing I said to the media), "but these idols are dead, whereas the God of Moses is still very much alive!"

There was applause.

The minister was exultant; I kept a very low profile, I even refused an interview with *Paris Match* because I only had a few days to carry out my plan. Now that pictures of the tablets were about to blanket the world, I had to remove myself away from the political scene.

The minister had given me carte blanche, and the director of the Louvre's laboratory, Madame Auclair, bombarded me with questions. Was I officially making a gift of the stones to the museum? Who was the rightful heir? Might there not be fears that Israel could reclaim the tablets? Should Djibouti be telegraphed to confirm that the right articles have been received? Where should we begin the research?

The next morning, the two relics were transported by lab employees on a hydraulic wagon from the first floor to the basement where most of the restorative services are located. They were deposited in a huge room where the walls were crowded with old paintings and where skilled artisans were bent over their work like monks in a monastery. With large-scale photographic equipment, we took life-size pictures. X-rays showed nothing unexpected, a technician made reproductions of the divine text, placing sheets of rice paper over the stones, which he had first inked, using the tablets to draw sublime lithographs. Another technician tried to clean the letters with a small brush, but the acid was threatening to destroy them.

"Can we date these stones through Carbon 14?" I asked the director, hoping to seem slightly knowledgeable. I should have held my tongue. In earlier days, Rodriguez, with reason, often used to remind me to keep silent.

"The Carbon 14 method, you know," Madame Auclair replied, "only allows precise dating of animal or vegetable remains. Your stones contain no CO_2 ... They've never eaten anything!"

Without thinking, I shot myself in the foot by pressing ahead: "What about strontium, or potassium, or radium, or other techniques for ..."

"I think these stones are several million years old; they're pre-Columbian, but that's not what you want to know, Monsieur Larochelle, what interests you is the age of the

lettering. It could be five thousand years old or five hundred.
It's impossible to compare Moses's style on the tablets with
other artifacts, you see."

God's words had to be taken at face value. It was the phil-
ologists' turn now to tackle the case. They spent two days
arguing.

I was already at another stage. At eleven o'clock that
morning, I crossed the esplanade toward the Louvre's ticket
booths. I had detected a building occupied by antique dealers.
These boutiques in the Rue de Rivoli, near several luxury
hotels, offered gilded knick-knacks and renowned artists'
paintings, Persian rugs, and Khmer statuettes (whose reputation Malraux had assured) displayed in armoires of carved,
honey-coloured wood. Each antique dealer specialized, more
or less, in a period or category, this one china and silverware, that one antique dolls. It would be surprising if I
couldn't find a cousin of my Djiboutian Antiquarians among
these merchants, a dealer with an elastic conscience ready to
offer his services for cash. Paris smelled of dust, smog, and
diesel fumes. The walls of the Louvre, opposite, were grey
like the underside of the sky. The doors were just opening,
the merchants were lighting their shop windows, one of
them had a display of old muskets with crescents on their
ivory butts.

I entered his shop looking like a conspirator, with the
collar of my trench coat turned up, but without hiding my
cassock. To give myself a touch of class, I picked up a vase

that Plato must have owned and slipped him my message while putting it back down on the counter.

"I'm interested in two stones, relics of Moses who ..."

No need to elaborate further, *Le Figaro* was open on the counter, and the shopkeeper had been reading the paper's article on the tablets. I pointed at my head; in the press photograph, I was standing on the left behind the minister. The man had recognized me.

"You're the hero of the day, Father," he said, squinting as he looked at me. He should have been wearing glasses.

Blond, dressed up like a hairdresser, slightly shorter than I, he seemed to me a rather sturdy fellow.

"I'd like to recover my property," I stated very softly.

He replied in the same tone of voice.

"Don't think of it! Those stones belong to the Republic now."

We were whispering as if in a confessional, although we were visibly quite alone in his lair. He had a thick moustache, which helped him be discreet, and his waxy complexion so accentuated his wrinkles that, all told, he seemed himself to belong to the world of ancient objects.

"You and I both wish the good of humanity ..."

"And who's telling me that Moses would be better served by you than by the state?"

"It's the Jesuits who are paying, and you know our funds are inexhaustible."

"I'm not of your religion."

"D'you think I'm having fun tooling round Paris in a cassock?"

Finally, he laughed, he was weakening, adding that without an accomplice he could not enter the galleries. I showed him the identity card Madame Auclair had given me and assured him that I had the entry code.

"I will be your accomplice, but we have to act fast, by surprise."

We talked a long time to agree on the price, half in advance, the rest on delivery, I promised to draw up a plan of the doors, windows, corridors, and elevators of the section of the Louvre where his men should get inside. They had to be quick, taking advantage of the tablets being in the laboratory.

I went to get the necessary money on Rue Scribe near the Opéra, at the American Express office where my card allowed me to borrow any sum I needed. The bill would be sent to the Company's accountants, then forwarded to the Emperor. Someone was sure to find the sum exorbitant. I took advantage of being here to make a phone call, there were too many customers and too much business being done in this office for the Amex telephone booths to be bugged. I wanted to say goodbye to Marie-Louise.

"Hello, Marie."

"Hello," she replied with restraint.

"Don't you recognize me?"

"My defrocked priest! How are you? What are you doing?

Are we going to get together soon? Papa's delighted, you know, with this whole business."

"And I'm delighted to have met you."

"Are we going to have lunch?"

"Not possible. I'm leaving town again. This time to sort things out in my mind."

"You're going into retreat?"

"I'm negotiating my exit."

"By the way, you were right about Timothy Leary. He's fascinating. He's a clown and a prophet both at once. I went to hear him at Nanterre. While he was talking, his disciples were distributing LSD! The cops intervened and arrested him."

"You don't do things by halves in Paris."

"On Saturday, there's a demonstration at the Bastille."

"Take Papa with you!"

I gave her a kiss. I was spending my life giving kisses over the telephone.

I didn't embarrass Marie-Louise. I didn't even embarrass the Republic. There was not a word in the press about the disappearance of the Tablets of the Law from the Louvre. Foreign Affairs had examined the situation and concluded that either the Negus's henchmen or Israel's myrmidons had decided to take back the relics. At no price did the French government want a war over the tablets, which, meanwhile, were travelling by truck-and-trailer to the southwest, where I received them. The Louvre was in total confusion, Madame

Auclair was at her wits' end, and I took off in seeming despair without leaving an address.

People still think to this day that in a few months they will be able to touch the stones in the museum, once the conservators have finished their work of restoration. The conservators hadn't conserved anything, even the photographs, which had been turned over to the archbishop of Paris. Rome hesitated before realizing that the tablets were back in my possession. The Superior General admitted to me that he had spoken to the minister. Paris gave the green light for me to be tracked down, but Paris mistrusts Rome, Rome mistrusts me, now all that's left for me is to mistrust the police.

The general delivery at Lourdes is located at the foot of the Black Prince's Hill and bears his name. How my father would have loved this novelistic dimension! I decided to wear a dark blue English jacket and grey pants; with a cap on my head I walked past the post office, trying to spot an agent on watch. Postal customers were going in and coming out in a continuous stream. I retreated to a smoke-filled watering hole opposite, I ordered a beer, I waited patiently, I would have to do it with nerve or send an intermediary. I decided to do it myself.

The clerk behind his wicket had a face almost as yellow as the postal notices on the walls, he was short of fresh air, like the Abouna in his chapel. I presented my passport, the envelopes were all bound with elastic, he sorted them quickly with fingers already ravaged by arthritis. In a few years he'd be going next door to soak his limbs in the water of Lourdes.

"Larochelle, Larochelle ... no ... ah, yes! Sign here."

The Black Prince's clerk presented a register upon which I placed my signature, I paid the required fee and retired to a corner protected from prying eyes. If I was going to be arrested, now was the moment. Or might the plan be to follow me? I was hesitant to open the envelope, I studied the Vatican stamp, gold and blue with the keys of Saint Peter. What was Rome replying?

Repent, Larochelle, and render unto God that which is God's!

The missive, on bristol card, was signed by the pope. How about Caesar, I thought, what's he going to live on? Repent! I wasn't guilty of anything, except for a time of having thought I'd outfoxed the Curia. Repent! I was infuriated.

I retrieved my car and headed for the freeway. To make sure I wasn't being followed, I left at a cloverleaf and came back on at the preceding one, then drove as far as Bayonne, watching in the rear-view mirror, before turning back to Biarritz. I didn't think it was possible for anyone to have followed me, I was being as careful as a wise old friar, but really, I was just a beginner, a choir boy.

It wasn't the post office where they came after me, it was the hotel. Someone had asked to see me, the doorman said, and would come back at five o'clock. The man had a strong

American accent and looked like a businessman, he added, pleased with himself. How had they found me? I decided to get out before my visitor came back. I asked for the bill. I cursed myself going up in the elevator, I'd been careless. There's always someone more Jesuit than oneself. I practically ran to my room and opened the heavy double doors in a rage.

Dougherty, sitting in an armchair, raised his left hand in greeting, the other held a revolver propped on his thigh.

"You're a sly little fox," he drawled in that unbelievable southern accent of his, "but I hang in there tighter'n a crab. The Jesuits use intelligence and finesse, I recognize that, but I'm the Labrador that sniffs out a trail step-by-step. Did things go well with His Majesty? Did you carry out your operation?"

"What are you doing here?"

"Rome telephoned Washington, and ol' Dougherty, who was getting bored on the coast, was offered an urgent job — to find a young Jesuit having a spiritual crisis and bring him back to the bosom of the Church. Where have you hidden Moses's Tablets?"

"What do you intend to do with them if I tell you? Take them back to Jerusalem? Sell them in Hollywood?"

"Don't be so disdainful, Larochelle, you're not the only idealist in the intelligence business. I'll deliver them to the Holy Father. Paris offered them to him. It will be a fantastic ceremony, I promise you. In France, the Catholics will be out of their minds, and all over the world they'll be on their knees.

Imagine God's Commandments beside the commandments of the Church, a great religious revival is going to sweep the West!"

"I thought you were a Protestant."

"It's not only Catholics who believe in God."

"I'm an agnostic. Your ceremony bores me in advance."

"You'll find faith," he retorted, a mite pretentiously.

"And you, how did you find me?"

"The credit network. You left your tracks at Europcar."

"We're not going to talk this way all day, Dougherty, couldn't you put away your gun? There's champagne in the fridge. Shall we drink to our getting together again?"

Puritan Protestants make the best secret agents and the worst friends. Dougherty was like a Labrador and a bulldog, too. He was stubborn, he insisted on knowing, wanted to get his teeth into something solid, not swill bubbles. I played my cards straight.

"The tablets are at Lourdes."

He burst out laughing.

"You're making bad puns, Larochelle. Now they're the Lourdes Tablets, that's 'Heavy Tablets' in English. I'm disappointed in you!"

"They're there, I swear it."

"It's Jesuitry," he snapped.

How could I convince him? I gave him this account to read and showed him the map of the site that I intended for the Superior General. He shook his head and finally believed me. I asked his permission to put on a cassock before we left, to put me in a spirit of reconciliation, I explained, but really because I had hidden a small bottle in the sleeve of the robe. Dougherty was not going to stop me from carrying out my plan.

We went to get the Lancia in the parking lot. The American had all kinds of trouble squeezing himself into the seat and buckling his rolls of fat under the safety belt, manoeuvring with his left hand and holding the revolver in his jacket pocket with the other.

"You wouldn't lend me a Swiss knife, would you?" I tossed at him as I started the car. He had no more inclination to laugh than to drink. I left Biarritz with regret and concentrated on the traffic. Now he was the one who wanted to make conversation.

"It's not the first time an agent has decided to make off with the fruits of his labour," my watchdog said. "It's a shabby trick."

"I didn't make off with anything. I was claiming fair pay for my efforts and taking retirement from the Company."

"At thirty-five! Retirement, for Pete's sake! After all the Company has invested in you, have you thought about that?"

"*Ô Seasons, ô chateaux! What soul is pure as snow?*"

"Don't poke fun at me."

"I'm not poking it at myself."

Daylight was ending over the Pyrenees and the eternal snows were sparkling in the distance. We had passed Pau, and I was trying to look ahead to the next moves. The American kept watching me steadily as if, with a jerk of the steering wheel, I could have bounced him out into the begonias or the banana trees.

"Pretty area," he said, waving at the fields and hills.

"I would have settled here if you'd given me the chance. It's the country of Henri IV, who was sometimes Protestant, sometimes Catholic, sometimes even atheistic."

"You're going to have a lot to tell your confessor, you ungrateful Jesuit!"

"You have a profound inner life, Dougherty?"

"Yes. Of course. I converse with God every day."

"Well then, converse with him and let me drive in peace."

I could see clearly that he wasn't going to let go of me.

When we arrived at Lourdes, evening was falling and the crowd was blindly affirming its love of the Virgin Mary, Mother of God. The American's eyes filled with emotion. It was hard to find a parking place near the boutiques selling religious articles, rosaries and bottles of water, medals and flags, colour lithos and light-up crucifixes, steps away from the sanctuary, where the chants from the numerous loud-speakers covered the area with pathetic tones, but Christ was with us, and I was able to slip between two trailers come from Iceland.

Thousands of candle lanterns lit up the faces of the faithful as they moved in procession. We carefully cut through the crowd. I might have tried to lose Dougherty, but the CIA bloodhound with his mug like a brute's on the point of divorce would have found me. We skirted the steps of the ancient basilica and I guided him toward the shed.

"It's here," I said, opening the metal door with my little key. "Do you want to see?"

The entrance was low and narrow, he insisted I go in first, I curled myself up to enter the gardeners' storeroom. When Dougherty, in spite of his size, succeeded in passing through, I was waiting for him in the darkness and gave him a whack with a pickaxe that made him twist and scream. He dropped the gun, I shoved it outside and closed the door of the hut. Dougherty was writhing in pain, the pickaxe had gashed his head and forearm, he could give up his soul to music if he wished, the organ had taken over from the sanctuary choir in a baroque crescendo.

I untied the nylon ropes the antique dealer had used to lash the tablets, tore off the Ethiopian cottons, laid bare the words of Yahweh.

"Repent," I ordered Dougherty, "for not believing me, and see the words of your Creator here before your eyes!"

So saying, to be safe I gave him a great wallop in the belly with a spade and he was winded before beginning his rattling groans again.

"Do I hear you praying now?"

Turning away from the American, I took out of my sleeve the little bottle I had filched from the Louvre. I'd been treated with contempt. I chose now to deal religion a knockout blow by blotting out the Ten Commandments one at a time, beginning with the first and very conceited order to bow down to no other gods but one and ending with the injunction against coveting one's neighbour's wife. From one letter to the next, the acid ate away the stone, of which there would soon remain only blank surfaces. Naked granite. I eradicated the words of God and erased the style of Moses.

The heat was infernal, the unsuspecting crowd kept calling for miracles, thronging together, mere steps away before a grotto dotted with candle lanterns, hoping for an appearance that would never happen again. Candle lighters bustled around bins of candles that were selling for ten to one hundred francs, and whose flames were flickering like the morality of the century. We were on the route of the crusaders, but I had turned my back on Saint James of Compostela. It was Rimbaud who would have rejoiced, who had felt the acid burns of the Commandments in his very flesh.

In the early morning, when at last there were more birds than pilgrims singing, I bundled the account I'm completing at this moment in the Decalogue's fragrant wrappings, and kissed the stones which were now as bare as the asses of angels. When I left the shed, Dougherty was still alive, his wounds seemed deep but certainly not mortal. He'll always be able to boast, and it's no small thing, of having been there for the disappearance of Good and Evil, amid the mingled smells of sulphur and incense.

In the taxi that took me to the station, I removed my cassock and made a ribboned gift parcel of it, and posted it while I waited for the train for Spain, where I fully intend to visit the birthplace of Ignatius.

On the back of the bristol card I received from the pope, I scribbled: "*Ite, missa est*, General, let's agree that I didn't have the vocation."

I can readily imagine him, pacing back and forth in a fury on the rooftop terrace of the Gesu in the cool air of Rome, hands behind his back, jaw lifted, eye fixed on the dome of Saint Peter's, his mind as twisted as the columns of the baldachin, racking his brain for a subtle vengeance (we had a hand in the Inquisition, didn't we ...).

I think of Véronik. From the barracks of Addis, can she hear the lions of the Ghebbi roar when it's time for antelopes to go to the river? Is there even anyone who feeds them since the troubles, or have they been-left to devour each other the way people are killing each other in the streets of the capital?

Operation Rimbaud, like the poet, went wrong, the Negus Negushi lost his bet. Adieu, Moses!

ACKNOWLEDGEMENTS AND PERMISSIONS

The quotation on page 99 is a translation of the following:

Ô blanc chasseur, qui cours sans bas
A travers le Pâtis panique
Ne peux-tu pas, ne dois-tu pas
Connaître un peu ta botannique

Arthur Rimbaud. Excerpt from "Ce qu'on dit au Poète à propos des fleurs," Letter to Théodore de Banville, August 15, 1871. Paris: Éditions de la Pléiade, 1951. This excerpt translated by Patricia Claxton.

Jacques Godbout is one of the leading artist-intellectuals of Québec. He was born in Montréal and educated at Collège Jean-de-Brébeuf and the Université de Montréal. He is the author of numerous works of fiction, non-fiction, poetry, and children's books; included among this is *Salut Galarneau!*, which won the Governor General's Literary Award in 1967. In 2004, his novel, *Une histoire américaine*, was selected for Radio-Canada's Le combat des livres, the French-language version of Canada Reads! An award-winning filmmaker, producer, and scriptwriter, he worked for the National Film Board beginning in 1958. He founded the magazine *Liberté* and, in 1977, the Union des écrivaines et des écrivains québécois. For his contributions to literature, he has won the Prix Belgique-Canada (1978), and the Prix Athanase-David

(1985). In 1985, he was made a Chevalier of the Ordre national du Québec. Jacques Godbout lives in Outremont, Québec.

ABOUT THE TRANSLATOR

Patricia Claxton is a literary translator who has translated
the works of many Québécois authors, including Gabrielle
Roy. Her translation of Roy's autobiography, *Enchantment and
Sorrow*, won her a Governor General's Literary Award in 1987,
and in 1999 she won it again for her translation of François
Ricard's biography of Roy. She has degrees from McGill
University and Université de Montréal. A founding member
of the Literary Translators' Association of Canada, she was its
first president. Patricia Claxton lives in Montréal.

This book was typeset using *Perpetua*, which was designed in the 1920s. It was one of eleven typefaces created by Eric Gill.

The Harry Ranson Humanities Research Center in the University of Texas at Austin houses an Eric Gill Collection. It is comprised of a Print collection (type specimens, alphabets, and wood and stone engravings), a Drawings collection, and a Sculpture collection.

His works of sculpture were commissioned as decoration for the BBC building in London and the League of Nations building in Geneva, to name a few.